FALLING OVER SIDEWAYS

JORDAN SONNENBLICK

FALLING OVER SIDEWAYS

SCHOLASTIC PRESS
NEW YORK

Library of Congress Cataloging-in-Publication Data available

ISBN 978-0-545-86324-7

10 9 8 7 6 5 4 3 2 1   16 17 18 19 20

Printed in the U.S.A.   23
First edition, October 2016

Book design by Nina Goffi

To Emma, my wonderfully dramatic girl—I am so glad you never have to be a middle-schooler again! And to Ross, Emma's amazing big brother—I am so glad that when she was in middle school, she had you for support.

June 15

I'm waiting in the wings, watching all of the fathers dancing onstage. Well, all of the fathers except mine. It's my annual dance recital, and I have just turned fourteen. This is the first year I am old enough for the Dads' Dance—the big father-daughter number that closes the first act of the recital every year. I have waited since I was a little girl to be in this dance, but just because you've waited for something doesn't mean you'll get it.

All of the other girls around me are whispering, pointing, giggling as their dads ham it up in the bright lights of the theater. There is booming surf music playing, and at the moment, half of the men are pretending to water-ski, while the rest are acting like lifeguards, throwing Frisbees around, hula-hooping, and even flying imaginary kites. It's incredibly dorky, but also incredibly sweet. My eyes burn, and I step back into the shadows a bit. I don't want anybody to see me tearing up, but it's hard to be inconspicuous as I dab at my face with the corner of my ridiculous tiki-girl skirt.

My best friends at dance school, Alanna Salas and Katherine Byrne, notice, and drape their arms over my shoulders. This only makes the tears come faster. "I'm *fine*," I whisper, a bit more harshly than I mean to. They both pull away and give me that look—the sympathetic-but-doubtful one that everybody has been giving whenever I claim to be okay.

I have probably gotten that look ten thousand times since the morning last September when my father—and my life—tilted and slumped over sideways.

Alanna and Katherine let me go—or at least, they do after I shrug their arms off my shoulders—and for some reason, I think about when I used to go swimming with my dad when I was five years old. I was in half-day kindergarten back then, and my father, who writes novels for a living, quit his day job so he could spend three afternoons per week with me. We had little rituals for each day. Wednesday was pizza day. Thursday was movies. And Friday was swimming, which was the absolute best.

We would go to the indoor pool at the township community center, which was always basically empty at that time of day aside from us, plus some random elderly people swimming laps. There was a roped-off area for "free play." Dad and I owned that part. We played with floating cushions and kickboards and life vests and beach balls and every other toy and gadget the pool had. Before going in, we would stick our towels in the sauna so they would be all warm and toasty when we got out. After we were dried off, we would shower in the family changing room, and then my father would spend what seemed like hours trying to brush all the knots out of my long hair while I laughed and laughed at him. I always told him that Mommy never got the brush stuck in my hair, but of course that wasn't true. I'm pretty sure he knew that.

Finally, when my hair looked presentable enough, we would go home, make hot chocolate, and snuggle up together to drink it.

But none of that was the best part, the part that I will always hold close to me. The best part was when my father would challenge me to swim from the edge of the pool to him. I had taken some swimming lessons, but I wasn't very confident in my skills yet. Every week, my father would move a few steps farther out from the wall. Then he would say, "Come on, Claire! Swim to me! I have you!"

I would say, "What if I can't get to you?"

And he'd say the exact same thing every time. "Don't worry, honeypot. I will always get to *you*."

Some weeks, I would make him promise more than once, but always—always—I kicked off from that wall with all my might, paddled my little hands as hard as I could, scissored my legs, and headed straight for my father's arms.

My dad never once failed to catch me. But now things were different. Now my dad could barely even catch himself.

1. Cursed from Birth

(So, uh, Thanks for That, Mom!)

Almost a year before the Dads' Dance, at my thirteenth birthday party, I was lying on my back on top of my brother's old sleeping bag in our backyard. Alanna and Katherine were on my left, and my best friend from school, Roshni Shah, was on my right. We would have been stargazing, but the sky was entirely obscured by clouds, so instead we were staring up into darkness, although I could vaguely see my friends' faces by the light coming from the windows of my house. The wind was starting to pick up, and even though it was late June, the air was beginning to feel kind of chilly.

"Looks like we're going to get rained out again, Claire," Roshni said.

"Is this three in a row?" Katherine asked.

"Four," Alanna said.

"She's right," I said. "But actually, it's even worse than that. It's rained on seven of my thirteen birthday parties."

"Hey, yeah!" Roshni said. "I remember that time in elementary school when you had it at the community center, and there was all that lightning, and the food got soaked, and then all your presents flew away into the mud. That was pretty weird. Or in kindergarten when you had the *Wizard of Oz* party, and the Wicked Witch blew into the pool?"

"Wait, you're kidding, right?" Katherine asked.

"No, seriously," Roshni said. "Claire was furious when the witch didn't melt. She kept stomping her foot and shouting, 'This is *fake*!' It was pretty funny."

Then Roshni covered her mouth and said, "I mean, it wasn't *funny* funny. I'm sorry, I don't mean we were laughing at you at your birthday. It was just so . . . so . . . Claire-ish. Do you guys know what I mean?"

"Umm . . . I think so?" Katherine said hesitantly.

"Totally," Alanna said.

I couldn't believe I was being openly mocked at my own birthday sleepover. I turned sideways and propped myself on one elbow to glare at Alanna.

"What?" she asked. "You have to admit, you *do* have a tendency to be dramatic."

Just then, I heard the screen door open behind my head as I said, "I'm not dramatic—I'm cursed! I mean, come on! Don't any of you believe in fate? Let's review some basic facts. My perfect big brother was born on Presidents' Day—of course—and I was born on Friday the thirteenth. Honestly, what chance did I have in this world?"

My mom's voice floated over the lawn from the porch. "I noticed it was getting cool out, so I made some hot cocoa for you girls. Please feel free to come in and sleep in the family room, by the way."

"Mom," I said, gritting my teeth. "We are *not* giving up on sleeping out until it is actively raining. Maybe this will blow over. It would be kind of nice if, for once in my life, a storm actually did that."

"Whatever you say, sweetheart," she replied. "By the way, did I hear somebody say something about our Claire being a bit . . . dramatic?"

"Cursed, Mom. As you well know, since you were the one who chose to schedule a C-section on Friday the thirteenth. Who does that? I mean, besides witches and the undead?"

"What?" she said. "It was convenient. That way, we had the weekend for your grandparents to visit you in the hospital. You were such a sweet baby."

"Sweet, *cursed* baby."

"Okay, the sweet part didn't last very long, but we love you anyway. Good night, girls. The door is open, just in case it starts *actively raining*."

My friends and I have always had a tradition of making

goofy short movies at birthday parties, so while we were drinking our hot chocolate, we decided to use our flashlights and phones to film a scary clip. Pretty soon, we were all taking turns running around the yard, shrieking and howling. With the moonless night, the wind, and the feeling of the storm rolling in, the whole thing was absolutely perfect.

Until my brother came home.

I was right in the middle of improvising what I felt was a devastatingly brilliant werewolf song with Roshni, when the screen door banged open and Matthew barged into the scene. "What are you doing?" he yelled. "It's late, and I have early soccer training tomorrow! Go to sleep!"

My friends just looked at me like, *What is happening, and why is Matthew possessed?* I couldn't really help them out, because I was wondering the same thing. After several seconds of standing there frozen with my flashlight pointed up under my chin like a total moron, I managed to stutter, "But . . . but . . . it's my birthday!"

"It's not even your birthday," he said. "Your birthday was weeks ago. It's just your party. It's not like it's my fault you decided to wait until after your dance recital to celebrate. And it's not like I'm sending your friends home. I'm just asking you all to stop running around and embarrassing our family in front of all the neighbors so I can go to bed."

My father opened the door and both of my parents walked out onto the increasingly overcrowded porch. If many more people joined us, we'd have to apply to the township for some kind of special zoning permit.

"Tell her to—" Matthew blurted.

"Tell him to—" I started to say, reasonably.

"Claire won't be quiet, and I need to be on the soccer field at seven a.m."

"Matthew, please go inside," my mother said.

"But she—"

"I'm sure your sister and her friends weren't trying to offend you, Matthew. They were just having fun. But we'll talk with them about settling down, okay? Now go ahead in and get ready for bed. You don't want to have a big fight on your little sister's birthday, do you?"

Matthew turned around and went in, but I'm pretty sure he muttered, "It's *not* her birthday," as the screen door swung shut behind him.

I said to my friends, "You know what Matthew should have gotten me for my birthday? A big banner for my door that says CLAIRE GOLDSMITH: BETHLEHEM, PENNSYLVANIA'S #1 MINOR ANNOYANCE FOR THIRTEEN CONSECUTIVE YEARS!"

Mom said, "I think they were out of those at the store."

Dad added, "But you shouldn't put yourself down,

honey. I'm sure your brother doesn't think of you as a *minor* annoyance. Now good night, sweetheart. Good night, girls. Try to keep it down. Because if you don't, we might have to send Matthew out here again. Mwa ha ha ha!"

When my parents were back inside, my friends and I got ourselves comfortable in our sleeping bags and whispered about random stuff for a while: what eighth grade was going to be like, our embarrassing families, the worst things that had happened at everyone else's birthday parties. Roshni fell asleep first, so only my dance friends and I were awake. That's when Alanna whispered, "So, uh, what did you guys think of the email?"

"Umm, what?" Katherine asked.

"You know, the email from Miss Nina? All the moms got it yesterday. I've been dying to talk to you guys about it!" Miss Nina is the owner of our dance school. I got a sick, nervous feeling in my stomach. If my mother had gotten a major email from Miss Nina, I was pretty sure I'd know.

By now, all the lights in the house were off, so it was basically pitch-dark outside, and I couldn't see Katherine or Alanna at all. I wondered whether Katherine looked as nervous as I suddenly felt.

"Uh, Alanna, what does the email say, exactly?" I asked.

10

"Well, the beginning is all about how much hard work we've done this year, how much we've improved, blah blah blah. Then it says we're being moved up to the high school group a . . . whole . . . year . . . early! Can you believe it?"

I could believe Alanna was being moved up. She is an amazing dancer. We started together at the studio when we were little kids, and Katherine started a few years later. We all loved it from the start, but Alanna has incredible natural talent. I have to work super hard all the time at home for every little bit of improvement, and of course Katherine has been playing catch-up, since she started after we did. Alanna works hard, too, but when she dances, it never looks like she's working.

It looks like she's flying.

For the longest time, Katherine and I didn't say anything. Now I was glad I couldn't see my friends' faces, and that they couldn't see mine. Then, finally, Alanna said, "Uh, well, I'm sure your moms just haven't checked their emails. Or something. Right?"

"Right! That's probably it. I guess?" Katherine said.

Nobody said another word for what felt like hours. Alanna's breath deepened and slowed. I almost jumped when I felt a hand poking my sleeping bag. "Claire," Katherine said sleepily, "it will be okay. Right?"

I worked one hand free of my bag, reached out, and found hers in the darkness. "Sure," I said, squeezing her cool fingers. "It's dance. And it's us. How bad can it be?"

I lost track of time, but I know I eventually fell asleep.

Because when the rain and thunder finally came, they scared the heck out of me.

2. If There's a God, He Has Forsaken My Middle School

(Plus, Why Is He a *He*?)

I always get a gigantic zit right near the tip of my nose when I'm about to get my period. It's like a built-in warning light, but more painful and disgusting. So naturally, on the night before my first day of eighth grade, I looked in the mirror and noticed the cherry-red Queen of All Acne Land holding court in the exact center of my face.

Apparently, I hadn't had enough to be self-conscious about yet. Over the summer, I'd gotten contact lenses to replace the glasses I'd worn since the third grade, which meant I would be facing a whole makeover review board based on just that alone. Then there was my schedule, which had come in the mail the day before. As kids compared schedules by text and social media all day, I had found out that Roshni was basically the only person I really liked or trusted in my homeroom, which was a big deal, because in our school, your homeroom traveled with you to all of your major classes. Then there were two girls, Jennifer and Desi, who were sort of okay. I mean, they were the kind of girls who are fun to be around ninety-three percent of the time, until they suddenly and randomly say nasty stuff about people for the other seven percent of the time—I never knew when it might be my turn to get the seven percent treatment. I could hang out with them, text with them, and stuff like that. I just couldn't trust them.

The rest of the homeroom was like the group you'd put together if you wanted to shove them all onto a deserted island and then film an extremely dramatic reality TV show as they bickered, then fought, then eventually started killing one another off one by one. We had bullies and victims; we had kids of various ethnic groups who didn't usually mix well in our school; we had popular girls who were mean to everyone; we had band kids and jocks; we had nerdy Boy Scouts and wild party boys; we had an extremely smart boy with autism, Christopher Marsh.

And then there were the teachers. Every single one of them had taught my genius-role-model-of-a-student older brother three years before, so that meant they would all make comments about how wonderful it was to have another Goldsmith in class, and how wonderfully they knew I'd do. This would accomplish two things: put me under stupendous pressure, and make everybody else in the class despise me for sucking up—even though all I had done was show up and have a brother.

Aaaannnddd ... for the bonus round ... Satan was in my homeroom!

Picture the Lord of the Underworld. Eternal Tormentor of the Damned. Hissing, evil, catcalling destroyer of all things pure and good. Now shrink that bad boy down to about five feet and expand him greatly outward in all directions, and you've got Ryder Scott. He's been in my classes on and off since elementary school. You might even say we've grown up together, but—well—Ryder hasn't. His maturity level froze when we got to middle school, and he seems to have a special problem with tall, thin girls.

Like me, for example. We used to talk when we were little kids, but in the first week of band camp in sixth grade, he suddenly decided I was his worst enemy. And he'd kept it up for two years, which was why I was horrified when I found myself at a desk in the back of our homeroom, trying not to bend over and wince with each new wave of awful premenstrual cramps, and looked very slightly up to see Ryder staring daggers at me. With an immense act of will, I forced myself to straighten all the way into a sitting position. Like all predators, Ryder could smell weakness and fear.

"Hey, Storky, what a pleasure! Imagine us being in class together all day, every day. What are the chances? I'm a lucky man. How've you been the past couple of weeks? I went with my family to Costa Rica right after band camp ended in August. What did you do with the rest of your summer? I hope you didn't waste too much time practicing your saxophone, because no matter what, I'll always be better than you."

See? Charming, right? I hated when he called me Storky, because my worst fear was that I *did* look like a stork with my incredibly long legs. My dance teachers always told me how much I'd appreciate having long legs someday. My dad's mother, whom I call Gram, once went on and on in front of the whole family about how long and beautiful my legs were, and how men love long legs. I was eleven. It was disturbing.

I didn't say a word to Ryder. My parents had been urging me to ignore his attacks. They said he was just insulting me because he didn't know a better way to get my attention. My parents were nuts. Ignoring him didn't work. It just made him try harder to irritate me.

"And, hey, nice contacts. In case I didn't mention it during band camp, getting those glasses out of the way really allows your, um, complexion to shine through."

I tried to look right through him and say nothing. I even bit the inside of my cheek to stop myself from reacting. Then, a cramp hit, and I winced. Unfortunately, Ryder took that as a sign of victory.

"Lovely chat, Claire. We'll have to do this more often. How nice that we'll be together every period . . . of every day . . . all year!"

Then he walked away, laughing diabolically. Who actually *does* that?

Satan, that's who.

By third period, my cramps were so bad that they completely drowned out Ryder, my teachers' gushing over my wonderful brother, and even the angry throbbing of my zit. Plus, I was wearing my thin, white marching-band pants for the first-day-of-school pep rally, and I was starting to worry that I might leak through my pad.

I asked to go to the nurse, and my teacher asked me why.

NOW, THAT RIGHT THERE IS WHAT'S WRONG WITH SCHOOLS IN THIS COUNTRY! Obviously, everything about school was designed by men, and periods prove it. First of all, if guys got periods, I guarantee that our marching-band pants wouldn't be thin or white. No, they would be thick, deep-black rubber fishing waders with BIOHAZARD symbols all over them. Plus three layers of mesh lining inside, two outer layers of additional opaque plastic wrap, and quite possibly a morphine dispenser attached for bad cramp days. There would be several cots at the back of each classroom for boys who were experiencing any kind of period-related symptoms, and you wouldn't be able to spit in the hallway without hitting three Advil dispensers.

Second of all, the whole going-to-the-nurse system? Insanely un-girl-friendly. First, you have to lie to your teacher, because of course you're not going to say, "Umm, I think my pad is leaking," in front of your whole algebra class. The girls might giggle, but the boys would probably pass out and/or die. Then, when you get to the nurse and ask her for Advil, she asks you why you need it—again, right in front of everyone. So, you can either try to express your need through the clever use of mime, or lie again.

And if you need to go to the bathroom to deal with a tampon or pad? You need to be a freaking ninja. Think about it: You're not allowed to carry your purse around the school, because it probably violates some kind of Homeland Security anti-school-shooting law. But how are you supposed to smuggle your feminine hygiene products to the restroom without any kind of bag? Tape them to your leg? Hide them behind a loose wall tile in advance?

It's insane. One thing's for sure: By the time I got to both the bathroom and the nurse that first day, and got all my girl business taken care of, I was ready to go full-out ninja on somebody. Or I would have been, if not for the cramps.

The Advil kicked in around lunchtime, which was good because our cafeteria is already painful enough. I sat down at the very edge of my class's assigned table, because I felt like my brain would explode if I had to be in the middle of a crowd, and took out my lunch.

Ryder slammed his tray down right next to my spot and slid onto the bench beside me.

My first thought was *Roshni! Come save me!* My second was that I should have taken more Advil.

"What's up, my flamingo-like frenemy?" Ryder said with a smile. Ryder always called me his frenemy, as if I should be proud to be called that. While my kindergarten teacher was singing the friendship song, had his been teaching the class some kind of frenemy song? Ours gave out I'M A KIND FRIEND stickers when she caught us doing something nice. Did his give out little I'M A PASSIVE-AGGRESSIVE FRENEMY pins, perhaps when one child held the door for another but then let go a half second too early so the other kid's face got slammed? Or maybe when he got off the school bus, his mom asked him, "Sweetie, did you make any nice evil frenemies today? Would you like to tell me about it over some spoiled milk and half-burnt cookies?"

Anyway, I stared through Ryder like he hadn't said a word, and started eating my yogurt. Meanwhile, Roshni sat down across from me, but I didn't have time to feel any relief about that, because the toughest girl in our class, Regina Chavez, sat down next to her.

Speaking of frenemies.

"What's up, Ryder?" Regina asked. "Hey, Roshni. How was your summer? Did you go to India again?" Then she gave me a scary dead-fish stare and said, "Yo, Starbuck. Can I have some Skittles?"

Regina calls me Starbuck because I'm a white girl, and according to her, all white girls love Starbucks. I once asked her why she didn't call every white girl Starbuck, then. She replied, "'Cause I call *you* Starbuck."

I'm pretty sure Regina was in Ryder's kindergarten class.

I didn't want to get in a big argument with Regina, but I also didn't want to seem like a wimp—even though I was. My genius solution was to pass my little bag of Skittles around the group, which was mathematically a stupid move, because I only liked one-third of the people who'd be sharing them. Still, it was a little less embarrassing than just handing them all over to Regina.

Roshni took maybe five. Ryder opened up his peanut butter and jelly sandwich, and then poured a heaping pile of Skittles in between the bread slices. Regina held the bag for a moment, then laughed and passed it back to me.

"Don't you want any?" I asked.

"Nah. I just wanted to see what you would do, Starbuck."

The middle school cafeteria is basically a battle for survival, with forty-cent milks.

The last class of the day was science with Mrs. Selinsky. Matthew had never said much about her. All I knew was that he had gotten an A-plus in her class, and the only reason I even knew that was because he got an A-plus in every class. It would have been kind of nice if he had given me some kind of warning.

Because this lady was, well, odd. The first thing I noticed was that she had a million little tics. Her face twitched constantly, and so did her hands, her shoulders, even her whole head. Watching her was like watching a chicken, or maybe a very large pigeon. A very large pigeon that was in control of my science grade for the year.

Then she opened her mouth, and things went from odd to alarming. Apparently, she had an adult daughter who had been a perfect, sweet angel when she was a student. Mrs. Selinsky—"Call me Mrs. S, because I think we are going to have a lot of fun together!"—ranted for about fifteen minutes about how we should all strive to be like her kid. This was how we learned the class rules. The speech went something like this:

"The first thing you need to know is that I don't like slackers. My daughter, Meredith, was never a slacker in middle school. Just be like Meredith, and we'll get along fine. The second thing is, I don't like sneaky people. So don't be sneaky in here. When Meredith was your age, she *never* tried to get away with having two boys over when I wasn't home and then lie to me about it when she got caught. She never would have done anything like that. So again, be like Meredith. Third, I don't like messy people. Careless people. People who don't pay attention. Meredith was neat, careful, and attentive."

I hoped none of Mrs. S's students happened to be named Meredith, or they were going to be under a whole lot of pressure this year.

A few seats behind me, I heard Regina whisper to Ryder, "My big brother had this lady. She got him suspended twice, *for nothing.*"

"Which brother?" Ryder asked. "The one in the special class, or the older one?"

"The older one. She lied about him to the principal and *everything*. She'd better stay out of my face. That's all I'm saying."

"Oh, and one last thing," Mrs. Selinsky said. "I'd better not catch any of you talking about other people behind their backs. I hate that."

I looked around, and most of the class was just sitting there with their mouths gaping open. I wondered whether maybe someone had forgotten to give this woman her meds for the day. Or possibly the past several weeks. Fortunately, the bell rang for dismissal before Mrs. S could go completely berserk and actually start blowing us up with her lab equipment and chemicals.

Swell, I thought. *Only a hundred and eighty-four more days of middle school to go.*

3. Boots of Pain and Shame

A few days into eighth grade, I decided to wear new black leather boots. Technically, they were half mine and half my mom's, because she had said they were too expensive for just me to wear. Which would be kind of all right, except that then she had gone on to give a whole big speech about how I don't take good care of my things—right in the middle of the store. It was so typical. When Matthew started driving, she had said, "Your father and I know you'll take good care of the car, bud." When I wanted my feet to be covered and protected from the elements, I got the public lecture.

Usually, I fought back when she went on these rampages, but I really, really wanted the stupid boots. Forcing my voice to remain calm and steady, I said, "Mom, people are staring. Can you please be a *little* quieter?" Unfortunately, my mother is immune to embarrassment. It's like a superpower . . . a superpower I have *not* inherited. I get embarrassed by everything. And standing in the exact dead center of a wide-open department store shoe section while my mother went on and on about how "These are TWO-HUNDRED-DOLLAR BOOTS! You need to treat them like the fragile objects they are so they last a long, long time!" was completely excruciating.

On the other hand, they were two-hundred-dollar boots. And I got to wear them to school. I basically felt like I had to tiptoe everywhere I went, or encase my lower legs in bubble wrap, but, hey, we all have to make sacrifices for style.

I walked into homeroom with my head held high and my shoulders back, like a supermodel on a runway. Or at least I would have, if I hadn't been carrying my alto saxophone, my lunch bag, and a poster project, and if my backpack strap hadn't kept slipping down on one side and making me move like the Hunchback of Notre Dame.

But still, girls notice boots. Roshni gushed over them, and Jennifer and Desi said mildly appreciative things.

Then Leigh Monahan strode in, glanced down at my feet, wrinkled her nose, and said, "I *love* your boots, Clara."

"It's Claire."

"Whatever."

After she spun on her heels and walked away, all the girls just stood there and stared at me. My two-hundred-dollar boots had been judged, and now they were worth maybe half a bag of Skittles.

The silence went on and on, until finally Regina said, "Dang, Starbuck! Is it me, or did it just get cold in here?"

Sometimes my contacts would just suddenly start to burn and make my eyes water. I sat at my desk, looked straight down for a while, and wiped my face with my sleeve after I was sure nobody was looking anymore.

When the class had quieted down for the teacher to take attendance, a random boy who sat in front of me turned to another random boy and asked, "Uh, what just happened?"

The other one said, "What are you talking about? What just happened with what?"

"I don't know. All the girls were talking, and then Leigh said something, and they all got quiet and weird. It was spooky—like a showdown, but with no weapons."

"Dude, they're girls. Don't worry about it."

The rest of the morning, I felt like I should somehow cross my legs when I walked or something so the boots wouldn't be as visible. I knew it was stupid, and that Leigh lived to make other girls feel bad, but I couldn't help it. It was like everybody was whispering about me. Then, on the way to lunch, I swung past the band room, and there was a notice posted on the bulletin board:

CHAIR AUDITIONS START NEXT WEEK!

SEE MRS. JONES TO SCHEDULE!

Instantly, I felt a cold, heavy lump in my stomach. Between all of that and the misery of walking down the hall in my stupid, embarrassing Boots of Pain and Shame, it was pretty amazing that I didn't just collapse in a heap.

Chair auditions were a huge problem, because I was the second chair alto sax, and Ryder was the first. He was very paranoid that I might somehow be plotting at any moment to take his chair, so during the weeks leading up to the twice-annual auditions, he harassed me nonstop. Honestly, I was totally happy being second chair, but Ryder would never believe me. Ryder lived for the saxophone, but I played in band only because my parents had made me pick an instrument in third grade, and I'd randomly selected the alto sax because Matthew had said it was the second-coolest instrument, after trumpet— which, of course, was his instrument. And there was no way I was going to pick the same instrument my brother already played.

It was just my luck that Ryder had picked the alto sax, too.

Anyway, Ryder was irritating enough without chair-audition madness on top of his usual awfulness.

I shuffled and hunched my way into the cafeteria, whispering to myself, "Maybe he hasn't seen the sign. Maybe he hasn't seen the sign. Maybe—"

"You'll never beat me, Goldsmith! I'm the *man*. I signed up for the very first slot. I've been practicing scales for weeks. I know all our parts by heart. My tone is better than yours. My intonation is better than yours."

"Your humility is better than mine."

"My humility is better than—oh, I get it. Ha-ha. We'll see who's laughing when I'm first chair."

"Uh, you're first chair now. Is it making your life complete? Are you totally happy?"

"Ah, psychological warfare. Very clever. You'll still never defeat me!"

"I know, Ryder. That's why it's a good thing I don't base my self-esteem on how well I blow into a little tube with a bamboo strip attached to it." *No*, I thought, *I base mine on whether some evil lizard girl in my homeroom smiles upon my footwear.*

. . . .

Dinner that night was a battleground. First, Matthew spent twenty minutes or so telling our parents how great he had done at his soccer practice, how awesome his grades were, how one of his teachers simply insisted on moving Matthew up into the highest honors level—oh, and how amazingly things were going with his perfect girlfriend.

I concentrated on chewing and swallowing without gagging.

Then my mother turned to me and, instead of asking how my day had gone, she led off with, "Sweetie, do you want to explain why you *threw* our two-hundred-dollar boots in the corner when you got home from school today?"

I muttered, "I didn't throw them. I just kicked them off."

Mom sighed her big, dramatic "My daughter is being dramatic" sigh. Which is ironic, if you stop and think about it. "And *why* did you just kick them off?"

"Because," I mumbled.

Then Dad stepped in. Dad was never a big fan of arguments at the table. "Claire, your mother isn't trying to start a big fight with you. She's just trying to understand what's going on. Did something awful happen today?"

I felt the blood rush to my face, and my contacts were instantly burning again. "Stupid Leigh Monahan said she loved my boots!"

"The horror!" Dad said. Then he looked at Matthew and said, "Should we round up the posse and ride her out of town on a rail?"

Matthew just looked up at the ceiling, because as a perfect high school junior, he was far too advanced to joke about my lowly problems.

I jumped up from my seat, knocking over my milk into what was left of my dinner. "You don't understand, Dad! That means she *hates* my boots!"

My father crossed his eyes and said, "Me simple caveman dad. Me no understand complicated girl sarcasm. Me only know how to throw and catch football with boy. Also, scratch self and burp."

"Mom!" I shouted. Well, I tried to shout. But it came out as more of a whine. I hate my voice when it does that. "Make Dad stop making fun of me. It's not funny!"

"Oh, honey," she said, "it's a little bit funny. Now let's clean up this spill, and then we can talk about something else. Ellen Scott told me you have chair auditions coming up in band. Are you excited?"

It would be hard to overstate how much I hated my family as I squeezed out the rag at the kitchen sink and proceeded to wipe up my milk.

I carefully avoided making eye contact with any of them.

4. My One Safe Place

One thing that keeps me up at night is the fear that the boys in my grade will never mature. Seriously, sometimes I look around my class, at Ryder making disgusting faces at me, or at the two random boys in front of me attempting to burp the Pledge of Allegiance, or at all the other guys hard at work, diligently drawing their private parts in the margins of each other's homework papers, and I shudder. What if video games, repeated brain injuries from sports, and genetically modified foods have destroyed their higher mental functions?

What if this is their peak level?

I mean, what if twenty years from now, I find myself trying to cook dinner with one hand, holding a baby in the other, when my husband walks into the house, so I say, "Hey, honey, did you stop at the store for milk?"

Then the man I have pledged to spend the rest of my life with says, "No, but I called my friend Kevin and he told me some *excellent* fart jokes. And hey, do you want to see what I drew?"

That's when I will sigh and say, "No, dear. I really, really don't."

My big break from all this is dance class. There are no boys within two years in either direction of me at Dance Expressions, which is a great relief to me. Plus, I love having separate friends there who aren't wound up in the massive drama of my daily struggles at East Side Middle School.

For weeks, I had been incredibly pumped for the first night of dance. Katherine and I had never gotten the email that Alanna got—the one about moving up into the high school classes. Over the summer, though, we both had taken a bunch of extra classes and individual lessons, so we were pretty confident that Miss Nina would reconsider the situation and then bump us up to Alanna's new level.

When we got our schedules by email the week before classes began, everything became a nightmare. Katherine had moved up to Alanna's level in all the classes we both took, but I hadn't. Now they were together, and I was left behind.

How was I going to get through the year without my two best friends, especially when they were together for everything? I had signed up for eight classes: tap, rhythm tap, ballet, pointe, lyrical, jazz, modern, and contemporary. The only two dances in which I had moved way up to the high school level were tap and rhythm tap, and

Katherine and Alanna didn't take those. And I hadn't gotten pointe class in my schedule at all. Apparently, someone must have thought I wasn't ready to go on pointe, which is basically the biggest moment in a dancer's life. A dance confirmation. Dance bat mitzvah. Sweet dance-teen. Quince-dance-nera.

This was like some cosmic joke, and I didn't like being the punch line.

I could see it in my head already: Katherine and Alanna would start hanging out full-time with the serious, competition dance girls, the ones who were home-schooled so they could take twenty hours of dance a week. Meanwhile, I would be stuck dancing with kids younger than I was, getting worse instead of better.

Two days before classes started, I called an emergency meeting on my back porch to discuss this tragedy over pizza. Katherine and Alanna were both too nice to admit this would affect our friendship, of course. They swore we would be best friends forever, that we would all be in the same classes again in a year or two anyway, that we could still hang out in our free time. It was even possible that Katherine might have worked up a tiny, semi-real tear in one eye when we hugged each other after finding out about this stuff. But I wanted to scream, *Give me a break! You're going to have a million in-jokes I don't get, your gossip won't mean anything to me, and you won't care about my little-girl stories when you're up in the high school world.*

Plus, what the heck had the extra classes and lessons been for? I had wasted my summer in a blazing-hot, non-air-conditioned sweat lodge of a studio, busting my butt to prove myself worthy to the exalted Miss Nina. I had stretched when she'd told me to stretch, and planked when she'd told me to plank. I had spent half of July and August squatting in front of a wall, strengthening my core muscles.

I was a strong, stretchy, well-cooked failure.

That first night of class, which fell on a Friday, was the most humiliating thing ever. The higher-level pointe class started fifteen minutes before my ballet class, and my mom had to drop me off early because she had some kind of back-to-school meeting to attend. So there I was, making small talk with all these girls I used to be in class with when we were little, and probably half of them thought I'd be going into their studio with them. Katherine and Alanna wanted to know how Roshni and I were doing at school—because they both go to a different middle school across town from mine—and I made them laugh by recounting some of the horrors of Mrs. Selinsky.

I was jumping up onto a chair and shrieking, "Be like Meredith!" when Miss Nina stepped out into the hallway and gestured for the older girls to come in.

It couldn't have been more awkward if I'd been shout-ing, "Go on without me!" and wearing a dunce cap.

The awkward, immature fifth-through-seventh-grade girls who made up the majority of my new dance class group started wandering into the waiting room. I know it was unkind, but of course I was sitting there thinking, *I'm better than you, I'm better than you, I'm better than you* . . .

Even my teacher, Miss Dana, must have thought so, because when she saw me in the room, she asked, "Claire, what are you doing here? Shouldn't you be in my Tuesday Advanced Two class with Alanna and Katherine?"

It was amazing. We were standing in front of the full-length mirror at the ballet barre, so I could see a blush spread across my entire head and shoulders in the course of maybe half a second. I managed to choke out, "I don't know. This is where Miss Nina put me, so here I am." It might have come out a little bit snarky, but I wasn't trying to be. Mostly, I was trying to keep my voice from cracking.

Miss Dana told us to start stretching, and then she said, "I'm going to see about this. It just *can't* be right."

I did a bunch of calf stretches and lower-back work while trying to ignore the glances I was getting from half of the other girls in the room. Depending on whether they knew how old I was, I was sure they were thinking either *Who does she think she is? Why should she get to move up?* or *What did she do wrong to get stuck in such a low group?*

When Miss Dana came back in, she took me aside, put one arm around me, and said, "I'm sorry, Claire. You *are* supposed to be here. I guess we'll just have to make the most of it. I mean . . . you'll just have to make the most of it. I'm glad to have you. Again. I mean . . . uh, we'd better get started."

The thing about being thirteen is that every time you think life just couldn't possibly get more awkward, it proves you wrong. The awkward just keeps on coming. During the class break, I was doing my Algebra II homework while three of the other girls were huddled together working on long-division problems. Long division! I wanted to die. I was just waiting for them to break out some Dora the Explorer juice boxes and animal crackers so we could have a serious class party.

Katherine and Alanna were out at the soda machine right when I came out of a class. We said hello and everything, but I could hardly look them in the eye.

When the night ended, a few of the little fifth graders said good-bye to me in their chirpy little voices, and Miss Dana gave me a sympathetic look. I hung my head and slunk to my mother's car in shame. Mom asked me how class had gone, and I just buried my face in my arms against the window.

Dance had always been the one place I looked forward to going. I loved visiting the dance store and picking out my new supplies for the year. I loved the ritual of putting on my ballet slippers, my tap shoes, my foot undies (don't ask). But now it was just one more hellish gauntlet to walk through.

So when I walked into my house and my father said, "Hi, honey! How was dance?" I might have been a tad snappish with him.

"How was dance?" I spat. "I'll tell you how dance was! Katherine and Alanna spent the night with all the advanced girls, doing millions of fouettés across the floor and learning the secrets of high school, while I hung out with a bunch of prepubescent, four-foot-tall babies and learned how to do a freaking *leap* for the millionth time. I don't know why I bother showing up at that stupid place. I don't know why I bother doing anything! I am a gigantic, failing loser. You should see me in there. When I lined up at the barre with these girls, I looked like the mother duck leading her little duckies. You should probably just kill me now."

"So you're saying it wasn't that great, then?"

See, that was the thing about my father. He always joked at the worst times. When I was little, I thought it was really funny, but starting in about seventh grade, it just embarrassed me and made me mad. And then, when he saw me getting upset, he would joke more, because that was his standard thing to do when I was upset. It was a vicious cycle.

"Dad! I'm serious! I threw away my entire summer trying to impress Miss Nina, and obviously the only impression I made was that I am the worst dancer in the world. She probably would have put me in the toddler group except I'm already potty trained."

"See, it could have been worse. At least she took that for granted."

"I quit. I am not talking about this with you. You don't understand what it's like to struggle. Every story you ever tell about your childhood is about how you got the best grades without trying, or how you were the best drummer in the school. Well, I have to work really, really hard, Dad—and it still doesn't do any good!"

"Honey, I've struggled."

"Well, maybe you need to struggle some more!"

And that's how I ended my last normal conversation with my father.

5. What They Don't Cover in Red Cross Babysitter Training

If I had known I was dressing for the worst day of my life, I would probably have chosen black socks or something. Or at least avoided the T-shirt with the panda on it. As it was, on Saturday, September 10, I woke up in a great mood because there was no school. Then I practically skipped down to breakfast, looking all cute and girly, my hair in braids. Usually on Saturdays I was the first one to come downstairs, but my mother and brother were already out.

"Where is everybody?" I asked my father, who was sitting at the kitchen table, drinking tea and reading the newspaper. I remember noticing that he was using the SUPER DAD mug I had bought him for Hanukkah one year.

"Oh, you missed all the fun," he said. "Mom thinks your brother needs extra practice for his driver's test next month, so she woke him up at eight. We had eggs, bacon, a battle of wills—good times! I think there's some leftover bacon if you want to microwave it. Or, you know, eggs."

I made a face at him. My father knew I hated eggs with a burning passion that defied all mortal understanding, so he offered them to me at every possible opportunity. It didn't even have to do with the fact that I had been angry at him the night before—he just loved to torment me with eggs.

"I think I'm just going to make some *hagelslag* on toast." *Hagelslag* is basically chocolate sprinkles, but it's special imported chocolate sprinkles from Holland. My father once brought a couple of boxes home from a book tour when I was little, and ever since then, *hagelslag* with peanut butter on toast has been my preferred Saturday breakfast. And yes, I am aware that it is essentially just dessert.

Don't judge.

So I made my toast, Dad read, and we sat together and chatted about nothing, but also sort of ignored each other. It was just like a million other mornings. At some point, I got a text from Alanna, so I grabbed my phone, which led to me checking out what was happening on various social media sites.

I wasted my last twenty good minutes with my father, screwing around on the Internet.

Then, all of a sudden, the table lurched and banged into my ribs. I pulled away and shouted, "Ow! What the—"

Dad was standing up, leaning to his right. His mouth looked wrong, like it was melting on one side. "M-m-my tumble cat!" he said.

"What are you talking about, Dad?" My heart started thumping that scary thump in my chest, the kind where you feel like it's stopping between every two beats. The hair stood up on the backs of my hands, and our sunny kitchen suddenly felt cold to me.

He stared at me as if he was trying to send me a secret message with his eyes, and barked, "Muffin bat!" Then he sat down very hard, like someone had just swept his legs out from under him. He was still tilted strangely to the right, and I was afraid he would fall off his chair.

I didn't know what to do. I had taken Red Cross baby-sitter training classes, but somehow none of the simula-tion activities had featured a grown man falling down while shouting, "Muffin bat!"

It occurred to me that I was holding my cell phone. I dialed my mother's number, but got her voice mail. This was awful, because my father had complained for years that my mom never answered her phone. I had probably heard this speech from him a thousand times. "One day I'll be dying on the floor, Nicole. I will crawl on the floor . . . slowly, in great agony . . . to the phone. With my last, fading bit of strength, I will dial your number. And then I will gasp my last words after the beep."

Last words.

Holy cow. What was I doing? I had to dial 9-1-1!

It took me three tries, because my hands were shaking. When I got through, a calm, almost cheerful-sounding lady answered. "Hello, Lehigh Valley Emergency Center. Where is your emergency?"

I felt like I couldn't think. I felt like I couldn't *breathe*. "It's my dad! He can't—he's not making any sense. And his face isn't—"

"Miss, where is your emergency? I need to know in case we get disconnected."

"Eighteen Galloway Avenue, Bethlehem."

"Fluffin! Tat!" my father said.

"What is the number you are calling from?"

"Don't you have caller ID? I think my father is dying or something! Just come! Please!"

"Miss, we have to get all this information before we can send the help you need. Now, what is the—"

So I shouted my number at her.

"And what is the emergency?"

"Pumpkin over!" Dad chimed in. I noticed he had started to drool down the front of his shirt.

I was like, *My toaster is broken, you dolt! What do you*

think the emergency is? Or were you not listening to the whole "dying father" part? But I forced myself to stay calm and said, "My dad. We were eating breakfast, and he stood up, and all of a sudden, his face got weird-looking, and he keeps saying things that don't make any sense! Now, please come!"

"What is your name?"

"Claire Goldsmith."

"And you're a female?"

My mouth said, "Yes," while my brain screamed, OH MY GOD! Just shut up and send an ambulance!

"How old are you, Claire?"

"Thirteen."

"And you're the only person in the home right now, aside from the patient?"

"Yes."

"Muffin! Muffin! Mup!" Dad's eyes were wild now. He swung his left arm across the table in front of him, which knocked over his mug and sent tea flying everywhere. The mug shattered.

I shivered.

"Is your father conscious?"

"Well, his eyes are open, but he isn't making any sense. And his face isn't working right. Actually, one whole side of him isn't."

"Is he breathing normally?"

"I think so."

"Claire, I'm going to put you on hold for one moment while I dispatch an ambulance to your location. Then I am going to come back on the line and ask you some more questions. In the meantime, please try to keep your father calm and still."

I walked around the table to my dad's droopy right side and sat next to him.

"Daddy, I'm here," I said. My voice sounded shaky and weak. I hated it. He didn't turn toward me.

"Stuffing?" he asked, sounding sad. Then he turned as far away from me as he could and repeated it. Then I realized: He couldn't turn his head in my direction.

I scurried around behind him so that my face was next to his left side and we were eye to eye. Next, I placed a hand on his left arm and said, "I'm here, and an ambulance is coming. I won't leave you. I promise."

"Puppet!" he exclaimed. He looked a bit less frantic, so I knelt there, patting his arm and talking quietly. He had once found a stray puppy when he was out jogging, and brought it home with him. I remembered that the puppy was panting and darting all over the place, like it was panicking, so I gathered it into my arms and whispered to it until it fell asleep.

This was a lot like that.

The phone person came back on the line. "Claire, when exactly did this start?"

I looked at the clock on the wall. "It must have been about two minutes before I called you. Wait . . . I can tell you exactly." I clicked back through my phone's call log and saw exactly when I had called my mother. "Nine minutes ago."

"Does your father have sudden numbness or weakness of the face, arm, or leg?"

"Yes."

"Is he showing sudden confusion, trouble speaking, slurring of words, or trouble understanding?"

"Yes, definitely."

"Sudden trouble seeing in one or both eyes?"

"I'm not sure. But when I went on one side of him, it was like he couldn't find me."

"Sudden trouble walking, dizziness, loss of balance or coordination?"

"I think so. He sort of stood up and then tilted to one side."

"Sudden severe headache?"

"I don't think so. He doesn't really look like it hurts." *Thank God*, I thought.

"Has your father ever had a stroke?"

"A stroke?"

"A blood clot or a burst blood vessel in his head?"

My heart skipped. A stroke—of *course* that was what this was. I had seen enough stroke victims in movies and stuff that I should have put it together. But they were always old people. My dad was only forty-five. That was old, but it wasn't, like, grandparent old. It wasn't *stroke* old.

"No."

"Has he had any recent injury or trauma?"

"No."

"Does he have a history of diabetes?"

"No."

"Any other medical or surgical history?"

"Um, he gets migraines sometimes. And my mom is always telling him not to eat stuff because he has high cholesterol. And he had sinus surgery last year."

"Does he take daily medications for the migraines or the high cholesterol?"

"Yes."

"Okay, here's what I need you to do. The ambulance is about two minutes away. Can you gather all of your father's medications and put them in a bag? Then I will need you to open the front door of your house. Are you in a house or an apartment?"

"House."

"Good. Now, get those meds and open the door. I'll hold."

I ran to our front door and unlocked it. Then I grabbed a plastic bag from under our kitchen sink and swept all of my father's prescription bottles from the counter into the bag.

"Okay," I said. "I did everything you told me."

"You're doing a great job, honey," the lady on the phone said.

"Butter butt," my father said.

In the distance, I heard a siren.

6. Time Is Brain

A minute later, a big, heavy guy my father's age and a short, sweet-looking lady who didn't look much older than Matthew came up to our front door, wheeling a stretcher. "He's in here," I shouted from the dining room, where I had been patting my dad's back and whispering.

More specifically, I had been telling him a story about a memory. When I was really, really little—like maybe three or four—I had a round, soft plastic case full of plastic ponies. The ponies were all different sizes and colors, none of which were found in nature. We're talking hot pink, lime green, aqua blue . . . anyway, Dad and I used to play all kinds of imaginary games with the ponies. Then, at some point, he came up with a new game called FuFu, the Christmas Horse. For some reason, he would crawl around our family room in circles, making horsey noises, and I would chase him and shout, "I catching you! I catching you!" Sometimes, just when I was about to grab him, he would spin around, grab me, and say, "No, *I* catching *you*!" Then we would both fall over, laughing and cuddling.

Eventually, I would ride on his back around the room until he got too tired, and then we would pack up all the ponies in their plastic case for a "nap."

Telling him about all this seemed to help. His breathing, which had been kind of fast and ragged, slowed down, and he had stopped blurting out random words for a few minutes.

But as soon as the stretcher came into view, Dad got all hyper again and started yelling about mutts and bugs. The big guy introduced himself and his partner, and told me he would be evaluating my father while she got some background information from me. Apparently, he already knew our names from the lady on the phone.

As soon as she heard me talking with the medics, the dispatcher said, "I hear voices. Has the ambulance arrived?"

"Yes," I answered.

"Okay, then, Claire. I have to go handle other calls, but your father is in great hands. Good luck." And that was it. I was alone in a room with my dad and these two strangers.

The big man, whose name tag read BIL with one *L*, said, "Claire, here's the deal. We suspect your father may be having a stroke, which means we're in a big hurry to get him to the hospital. I'm going to evaluate him as fast as I can while my partner, Kathy, is talking with you, and then we'll load him onto this stretcher, get in the ambulance, and get going. Is there another adult around?"

"No, it's just me. And I can't get my mom on the phone."

"All right. Then you'll be coming with us to Lehigh Valley Medical Center. Now, let me ask your father some questions." With that, he knelt down next to Dad's chair and turned it so that Dad was looking at him. "Sir," he said, "I'm going to be asking you to do some things for me, all right?"

Dad just stared at him blankly. It was awful.

"Sir, can you give me a big smile?"

Dad didn't respond to that at all.

"All right, can you please lift both arms straight in front of you?"

Dad still didn't do anything. Well, he tilted his head and drooled, but I wasn't sure that was in response to the question.

Next, Bil asked Dad to repeat a tongue twister. I was thinking, *Really? He can't smile or raise his arms, but you think he might be up for a nice round of verbal challenge games? Maybe next we can try a game of Clue, although I suspect you guys might have an advantage.* I had to look away, which was good, because I suddenly realized Kathy was sitting in front of me, holding a clipboard, waiting to ask me a question.

By the time Kathy was finished going through a bunch of stuff about Dad's age, his allergies, his medications, and what I knew of his medical history, Bil had stopped trying to get Dad to do things and was about to prick his finger with a needle.

"What are you doing?" I asked. "Why aren't we on the way to the hospital already?"

"This is the last thing. I'm checking his blood sugar. Sometimes low blood sugar can look just like a stroke. If his blood sugar is low, we'll give him a quick dose of sugar, and he just might come around. If his sugar level is normal, we go."

Bil pricked a finger on Dad's right hand. Dad didn't even flinch.

I sat there counting seconds and praying for my father to have low blood sugar. I didn't even know what that would mean—diabetes? Kidney failure? But I knew that almost anything would be better than a stroke.

When my count was up to sixteen, Dad lurched to the right and bleated, "Mup! Muuuh!"

At the same time, Bil looked at something in his hand, shook his head once, and said, "Let's go." In thirty more seconds, tops, he and Kathy had managed to lift and strap Dad onto the stretcher and wheel him out of the house.

I grabbed Dad's meds, my house key, and my phone, and locked the door behind us. As I followed the stretcher, every hair on my body stood on end, and I wanted to cry. Or scream. Or grab on to the stretcher and not let them take my father away. I know this is crazy, but putting him into that ambulance seemed like an ending, like something you could never take back. People who got taken away from their homes in ambulances sometimes ended up living in rehab places forever. People who got taken away in ambulances sometimes *died*.

I wondered whether Dad would ever come home again.

Bil got in the back of the ambulance with Dad. Kathy told me to get in front with her, and as soon as my seat belt clicked, she hit the lights, the siren, and the gas pedal. There was a sort of mini wall between the front of the ambulance and the part where my dad and Bil were, but I could turn in my seat and see them through a little connecting window, which was open. Bil was talking to someone on the radio thing with one hand, and doing things to my father with the other.

I heard him say, "Suspected blah blah blah stroke." The middle part was a scary scientific-sounding word. Then he said, "We're now twenty-nine minutes past initial symptoms. Patient is awake and alert, but nonresponsive to verbal commands. Vitals look good. I'm hooking up the EKG now. I'll have two lines running within the next couple of minutes. Can you get the stroke team ready? We should be there in, uh, fourteen minutes. You're going to want to clear the CT scanner—patient failed the FAST test. No history of stroke. No heart history. No blood-thinning meds. No recent surgery, just some kind of sinus operation last year. History of high cholesterol. I'm going to guess he threw a clot. Looks like a candidate for TPA to me. Can you tell the neuro? Okay, thanks."

It's amazing how much you can hear over a siren when you're really trying. And scared out of your mind. It probably helped that Bil was a loud talker.

I turned back around as Bil broke a long needle out of a paper package. I couldn't stand to watch him poking that into my father while zooming over bumpy roads at highway speeds. I asked Kathy, "Can I text my family?"

Without looking away from the road, she said, "That sounds like a very good idea. Now is when you have a little free time. Things are going to be very hectic at the hospital."

I sent a group text to Matthew and my mom:

In ambulance with Dad. I think he is having a strike. Going to K fun Valley Medical Center.

Then I read what I had sent, and added two more messages:

*stroke
*Lehigh Valley Medical Center

Stupid autocorrect. It would have been a disaster if my mom and brother had tried to find their loved one at K fun Valley Medical Center, where he was being treated for a strike.

When I had sent the last text, I asked Kathy, "What's going to happen when we get there?"

"Well, with a stroke, the saying is that time is brain. From the time a patient first shows symptoms, we have only three hours, tops, to get a whole bunch of stuff done. We have to figure out for sure that the patient really is having a stroke, then find out what kind of stroke the patient is having, and *then*, if the patient is having the most common kind of stroke and is eligible to take it, we start administering a clot-dissolving drug called TPA. Fortunately, you did everything right, and you live close to a great hospital. Lehigh Valley is a certified stroke center, which means they shoot for a one-hour 'door-to-needle' time. If your father needs TPA, it looks like he'll have time to get it."

"Okay, but what are they going to do to my dad in this hour?"

"The big thing is that they're going to take lots of pictures of his brain in a special X-ray machine. It won't be painful or anything."

"And . . . is he going to be okay?"

This time, Kathy actually did look away from the road for a second to lock eyes with me, which would have been a lot more comforting if we hadn't been zipping past every car on the interstate. "I can't tell you that, sweetheart. But he's going to a place with a great team that specializes in treating the exact problem he's having, and we're getting him there as fast as humanly possible. Okay?"

I forced myself to smile back, hoping that if she saw me giving a positive sign, she would start looking back at the road. It worked.

That was why, when the tears started to slide down my cheeks, she didn't see them. All I could think about was what she had just said: *Time is brain.* I glanced back at my father, who now had an IV line hanging down into each arm, a bunch of wires attached to his chest, and a green line spiking up and down crazily on a monitor screen next to his head. His eyes were open, staring straight up, as though he couldn't see or understand any of it.

How much time did he have left?

And how much brain?

7. The Wet Read

At the hospital, things started to happen faster than I could handle them. The ambulance pulled up to the emergency room entrance, and Kathy jumped out before I could undo my seat belt, saying, "Come on," over her shoulder as she went. At the same time, I felt my phone vibrate. When I pulled it out of my pocket, it was Matthew calling, but I couldn't answer, because my hands were shaking too hard. I got half caught in the shoulder harness from the belt, and basically fell out of the vehicle.

Kathy and Bil were already pushing my father into the building, where a team of blue-gowned, masked people was waiting for them. I steadied myself against the side of the ambulance, managed to shove the phone back into my pocket, and ran to catch up.

I got there in time to see a man shining a bright light into my father's eyes. Dad whimpered. I would have whimpered, too, but this was different. Dad sounded like a hurt animal. I also noticed that even though the light must have felt awful to him, he didn't pull his head away or close his eyes.

The man said something about "positive pupillary response," and another guy typed that quickly into a little mini laptop. Dad grunted and thrashed his left hand around. His right just sort of flopped in place like a fish on dry land. Then the guy in charge started asking Dad the same kinds of questions that Bil had already gone through with him. I wanted to scream, "Leave him alone! Can't you see you're torturing him? He's not going to do your stupid nursery rhyme! Now help him!"

The man started reeling off a whole list of technical stuff that scared me. He was talking a mile a minute about "neural deficits" and aspirin and how Dad couldn't "protect his airway" and how they were going to have to "intubate" him.

At that point, an alarm went off right next to Dad's head. "His pressure's dropping!" the computer guy said. "We're going to need to get a CT scan, stat!" the boss said. "Tell the radiologist I'll be waiting here for a wet read."

The next thing I knew, a lady grabbed my arm and led me away from my father. I wanted to reach out and squeeze his finger or something, but I was afraid to touch a wire or a tube, or that I would hurt him. And then before I could think any more about it, I was getting pulled through a set of double doors into a waiting room, and Dad was getting pushed in the opposite direction down a long hallway, gathering speed.

As the doors swung closed, I whispered, "Bye, Daddy."

The lady who had brought me out was pretty rude. She asked, "Are you related to the patient?"

Even in that situation, I was like, *No, I just like to hop in random ambulances for fun.* Then I thought, *I'll have to tell Dad that one later.* Then I realized I had no idea whether my father would ever laugh at one of my smart-ass remarks again, and my whole body felt like somebody had dipped it in ice water. I guess I had been shaking the whole time, but suddenly, I was actually shivering. My teeth were rattling together and everything.

The rude arm-grabber lady repeated her question, and I said, "I'm-m-m hi-hi-s da-daughter. I-I-I . . ."

It hit me that I hadn't told any of the hospital people the exact time when Dad's stroke had started. The lady on the phone had said that was really important, and Kathy had told me that time was brain. "Ma'am," I said, "I ha-have to t-tell somebody when my d-dad's stroke started. It was at nine-oh-six."

"We'll get to that, dear."

I forced myself to control my voice, and shook her arm off. "When? *When* will we get to that? You just dragged me away from my father. What if the people treating him need to know this right now? Go tell somebody!"

She just sat there and stared at me.

"Please!" I said.

But she made me go through all the same questions I had already answered for the phone dispatcher and Kathy again anyway before she headed through the double doors. When they closed behind her, I let myself lean back and shiver.

I closed my eyes and tried to tell myself that everything would be all right, but it was pretty hard to believe. My head kept flickering between images of my father's frightened face, his floppy right hand, his body on the gurney with tubes and wires sticking out everywhere, and finally, the doors swinging shut behind him. Eventually, I tried to call Matthew back—not that I had much new info for him—and then shut my eyes when he didn't pick up.

It felt like I spent a million years slumped down in that uncomfortable chair, but it couldn't have been more than a few minutes before Bil and Kathy came over to me with a Styrofoam cup of hot chocolate. They sat with me for a little while and tried to cheer me up by asking questions about my life. It was a pretty transparent ploy, and if one more adult called me *sweetie, honey,* or *dear,* I was going to hurl a chair across the room.

Still, the hot drink was nice.

Mom came charging in, with Matthew in tow. She immediately started spitting out questions at top speed. "What happened? Where's your father? Are you all right? Who are these people? Did you pay for that hot chocolate yourself?"

I was like, *Can we please focus, Mom?*

Bil started to talk, but just then, a walkie-talkie thing on his belt started squawking. I heard something about a multivehicle accident on Route 78, with casualties. He grabbed the thing, pressed some kind of button on the side, and barked, "Twenty-seven responding." Then he jumped up and started walking away.

Kathy said, "That's us, honey." I was like, *I figured that part out.* She squeezed my shoulder and said, "We'll try to check in with you when we get back. Hang in there." I felt a lump in my throat. Kathy and Bil had both done a great job, as far as I could tell, but more than that: They were nicer than they had to be.

My mom said, "Claire?"

It all came out in a rush. "We were eating breakfast. Daddy jumped up and smashed the table into me. And then he couldn't talk right. He kept saying 'pumpkin' and 'muffin.' He was leaning to one side, and his arm wasn't working. So I tried to call you, but you didn't answer, so

I called 9-1-1. You didn't pick up. Why didn't you pick up? Daddy needs you, and I was so scared!"

I started to cry, and Mom and Matthew both put their arms around me. Mom was trying to look reassuring. Matthew looked like he was trying to decide whether he should vomit or faint. Matthew had always hated it when anybody got sick.

"Oh, honey," Mom said, "I'm so sorry. I turned off my ringer because your brother was driving. And then when we finished and saw your message, we couldn't get you on the phone." Mom patted me on the back and tried to brush the hair away from my face. I hate it when she does that. I pushed her hand away, and turned to glare at her.

"Don't comfort me, Mom. I'm not sad—I'm mad. Daddy needed you, and you weren't there. He always *tells* you to keep your phone on in case of emergencies."

My mother took a deep breath. "Let's forget about that for a while, Claire. We have to concentrate on doing what we need to do for your father. Now, what have the doctors said?"

I took three deep breaths, like my seventh-grade play director always said you should do to clear your head before you go onstage, and tried to get the sequence of everything clear in my mind. Then I laid it all out for her.

As soon as I was done, she said, "So we really don't know what's wrong with your father yet."

I said, "What are you talking about? He's having a stroke, Mom!"

"We don't want to jump to conclusions, Claire Bear. Just because some of the medical personnel thought he had some stroke-like symptoms doesn't mean that's necessarily what's really going on. Maybe he's just having a new kind of migraine. Or . . . or . . . well, I don't know. I'm not a doctor. But until a doctor comes out and tells us it's definitely a stroke, I think we should all try to stay calm."

Matthew was sitting next to me, looking straight up at the ugly off-white ceiling tiles and hyperventilating. I looked down at my hands and noticed I was unconsciously clenching and unclenching them every few seconds. I was pretty sure the staying calm thing wasn't going to work for us.

Mom casually strolled over to the front desk and started giving them our insurance information, like this was a plain old office visit. As though my dad had a nasty splinter or the flu, as opposed to a bleeding brain.

My mom never believed anything bad was happening until she had conclusive proof, and sometimes not even then. When I was little and my dad's father passed away from a sudden heart attack, she kept saying he might be all right until my dad called from the hospital to say he was officially dead. When I had an asthma attack and had to go to the emergency room, she kept saying, "We can't be sure it's really asthma," even as the medical personnel were strapping the nebulizer mask onto my face.

I thought, *If somebody ran in here right now with a hatchet and chopped Matthew's head off, she would probably stand over the body and go, "Well, I admit this looks bad, but maybe it's just a really messy nosebleed."*

I felt really guilty for thinking it.

But then I was like, *Claire Bear? Really? Am I five?* And I got annoyed again.

Meanwhile, Matthew hadn't said a word. He hadn't asked any questions, or scolded me for not answering his call, or even complained about anything. He was still sitting there, staring upward, with a completely blank look on his face.

I reached out and put my hand next to his. He looked down at my hand, grabbed it, and squeezed so hard it sort of hurt. Then he turned to me, swallowed, and asked, "Was Dad in a lot of pain? Did he seem scared?"

I looked in Matthew's eyes and saw something that stunned me: They were full of tears.

"I don't know. I don't think it hurt, really. Mostly, I think he was confused. And, um, agitated. Like he didn't understand what was going on, but he knew he didn't like it."

When Mom came back, I asked whether there was any news, and she said, "Not yet. Apparently, they're still doing tests."

"But, Mom, you have to make them hurry! Time is brain! If he doesn't get TPA within the next"—I looked at my phone for the time—"seventy-two minutes, it's going to be too late!"

"What are you talking about, Claire?"

"It's a drug that dissolves blood clots. But it's only useful within the first three hours after a stroke. Please, Mom. They have to hurry!"

"Your father is with a whole medical team that specializes in stroke care. If he's having a stroke, I'm sure they know what to do."

"But—"

"But nothing. Waiting is hard, but sometimes there's nothing else we can do. Maybe we should try to distract ourselves. Do you want to play a word game? Names, maybe? Or Geography?"

I worked my hand out of Matthew's, stood up, and walked away to fill my empty hot-chocolate cup at a water fountain.

Behind me, I heard Matthew say, "Geography? Seriously?"

I was glad he was sticking up for me, but at the same

time, I felt sorry for him. If Mom was the one who never believed anything bad was happening, Matthew was the one who thought every little thing was a disaster. He must have been even more worried than I was.

As I came back, the lead guy who had been working on my father walked out into the waiting room. "Mrs. Goldsmith?" he asked Mom. She nodded. "I'm Dr. Raj Venkersammy. I am a neurologist on the stroke team here at the hospital. I need some information really quickly so that we can make an urgent decision with regard to your husband's treatment."

Then he went through Dad's medical history in incredible detail. If there was one thing I learned that day, it's that words like *hurry* and *urgent* don't really mean the same thing at a hospital that they do everywhere else. When he happened to look in my direction, I interrupted and mentioned the time when Dad's symptoms had started. The doctor asked Mom several more questions about that, and then sighed.

"What?" Mom asked. "What is it?"

"Well, it looks as though your husband threw a clot. A few minutes ago, we got the report on the wet read of his CT scan, and there is definitely an occlusion in his middle cerebral artery."

"What does that all mean?"

"A stroke, Mrs. Goldsmith. Your husband is suffering the effects of a moderate-size stroke. I will answer more questions later, but right now I have to get back in there and get him started on a clot-busting drug."

He turned on his heels and practically sprinted back through the double doors. Finally, somebody was hurrying visibly! Of course, that probably just meant my father was in really awful shape.

Mom sat down and started rubbing her hands together. It looked like she was trying to start a fire using her fingers for tinder. I had never seen my ice-calm mother look so agitated before.

"Well, Claire, it looks like your father is having a stroke," she said.

I had never been so unhappy to be proven right.

8. Blood Shooting Everywhere, Plus a Late Lunch

It is amazing how much your brain races when you literally have nothing to do. Matthew and I sat in that stupid little waiting room for hours. Mom came and went. Sometimes she got called away to answer questions at the desk, sometimes she talked with medical people, and sometimes she stepped outside the hospital to make phone calls. But we just sat there.

So, what *was* there to do? Well, we watched people. Believe me, there's some eye-catching people drama in the emergency department. We saw three different people barfing into little handheld basins that the check-in people had given them on arrival. We saw an old drunk guy with a gigantically swollen bump above one eye. Even from several seats away, he reeked of alcohol. There was an elderly lady with him, dressed in a filthy bathrobe and fuzzy slippers. She kept trying to hold an ice pack to his bump, but then he would yell at her, "I got this! I got this!" As soon as she let go, he would drop the ice pack, and the whole cycle would start again. Oh, and then there was the thumb dude. He was maybe twenty-five years old, with one thumb wrapped up in a huge, blood-soaked ball of gauze bandages. His thumb looked like a red Q-tip.

A nurse had walked him to a seat facing us from two rows away, and told him to keep applying constant pressure to the wound, no matter what. But once every twenty minutes or so, he would pull away a corner of the gauze to peek at his thumb. A half second later, a geyser of blood would go pumping straight up into the air, like an oil well in a cartoon. So he would clamp down again.

There weren't a whole lot of quick learners in the ER that day. Maybe the quick learners don't end up there, as a rule. Aside from my father.

Anyway, the casualties kept piling up, because about an hour after my mom and Matthew got there, Bil and Kathy's ambulance came screeching up to the doors with another right beside it, and tons of hospital people came hustling over from all directions to meet them. Several patients came zooming through on gurneys, and a few of them made our dad look like a "before" picture. We're talking tubes, monitors, bandages, splints, wires—one person wasn't even visible at all, because he (or she) was surrounded by so many rescue workers. Someone actually yelled, "Clear!" just like in a movie, and then, before I could see anything else, the whole bizarre scene went banging away through the Double Doors of Doom.

Matthew and I just looked at each other for a moment, and then he said, "Well, that looked uncomfortable."

I almost giggled. One thing about Matthew: He is a genius at the art of understatement.

At some point, my mom's parents showed up. After a round of extremely awkward, silent hugs, Grandpa Ken asked, "So, are you kids hungry? Can we get you some food? Your mom said you haven't eaten anything since breakfast." I asked him what time it was, and was completely shocked to learn that it was after two in the afternoon. I had been at the hospital for going on five hours.

But was I hungry? I hadn't even thought about it. I mean, I was in a room full of sick, puking, blood-gushing, dying people. The smell alone would have put me out of the eating business indefinitely on a normal day.

However, this wasn't a normal day. "Yes, please," I said. "But I don't want to go anywhere, in case our father needs us or something."

"Matthew?" Grandma said.

"Sure," my brother said.

"All right, we'll go up to the cafeteria and see what they have. I'd imagine there's some pizza or something."

We both said that was fine, which was another indication of how abnormal this day was. Usually, Matthew would have worried about the health benefits and nutritional value of his lunch, asked for fruits and vegetables, told our grandparents to be sure to bring him some milk for strong bones and teeth, and nitpicked in about ten different ways. But he just agreed to cafeteria pizza and went right back to sitting still.

Or not really sitting still. His leg was shaking up and down super fast.

When the doctor came out and said, "Mrs. Goldsmith?" Matthew jumped up like a rocket. I texted Mom, and she came back inside. We all stood there in a tiny, tense circle, staring at the man until he said, "You may see the patient for a few moments now. But then we are going to have to perform some more procedures before we can move him upstairs to the intensive care unit."

Intensive care? That sounded bad. Everything sounded bad. The night before, I had been screaming at him about my dance problems.

Dance problems. How pathetic was that? Compared to what had happened since I'd woken up, *dance problems* just sounded like a giant oxymoron. Like, newsflash: If you're dancing, there are no problems.

And—God! I had been screaming at him. The last major thing I had said rang in my head: *Well, maybe you need to struggle some more!* I was probably the worst person in the hospital. I was, potentially, the worst person in town. I thought, *What if strokes are caused by stress? I mean, what could be more stressful than having your awful daughter tell you she wishes you would struggle more?*

We followed Dr. Venkersammy through the chaos of the open ER area and into a small room with a glassed-off front. Dad was in a bed there, and a woman was standing beside him, checking all kinds of gauges and monitor screens. He looked much worse than he had before. His face was almost purple, and there was a big plastic tube jammed into his mouth, secured in place with strips of thick-looking tape. His eyes were slitted almost shut.

My father looked like an old, old man. You might have even said he was struggling.

Matthew let out a high-pitched whimper and stepped past me. Then he leaned over as far as he could and buried his face in our father's lap. The machines were making all sorts of hissing sounds, but I was pretty sure I heard Matthew say, "Daddy." It was extremely quiet and muffled by blankets, but what struck me the most was that Matthew didn't sound at all like himself. He sounded like a little kid.

I had this crazy thought: *Nobody's the right age today.*

Dr. Venkersammy told us we could stay for only a few minutes but that we should feel free to "speak with your loved one as though he understands you. He cannot say anything right now, of course, but that does not mean he is not listening."

I moved forward so I was next to Matthew, standing over our father's knees. I wanted to say something helpful or something brave. Something useful and mature. But nothing came. I stood and stood and stood there, but my lips wouldn't move. Mom stepped up from behind and put one arm around me and the other around Matthew. "It's all right, Claire Bear. Just say anything. Your father loves you. He'll just love the sound of your voice."

Her voice sounded like it was about to crack.

I tried to say something. But my throat was closed. I felt like someone had jammed something hot, dry, and sticky down into it—sideways. Dad looked right up at me. It was like he was begging me to speak, but nothing came.

The machines hummed, Matthew sobbed, Mom made reassuring noises, and I said nothing. Then the nurse said, "Okay, folks, I'm going to send you back out to the waiting room. Mr. Goldsmith's blood pressure is inching up a bit, so I have to call the doctor back in. Don't you worry— we're keeping a good eye on every little thing in here."

And that was it. Mom steered us out of the room. Halfway down the hall, my throat opened up, and I whispered to nobody at all, "I'm so sorry."

Back out in the waiting room, Grandma and Grandpa were standing over a takeout box. "Any news?" Grandma asked.

"Not really," Mom replied.

"Got your food," Grandpa said. "Hungry?"

"Uh-huh," Matthew grunted.

Swell, I thought. *My father has a stroke, and the rest of my family starts talking like cavemen.*

The waiting area had started to empty out, which was kind of a plus for eating purposes. We munched through our food in silence. The pizza was about what you'd expect from a hospital cafeteria, but, thankfully, Grandma knew my brother really well, so she had also gotten us two apples, two milks, and a bottle of grape juice to share. That was a huge plus, because even a cafeteria can't do too much to ruin milk, juice, or apples.

While we were eating, the strangest thing happened. My grandparents started chattering away with my mother as if nothing out of the ordinary was going on. I guess they were probably trying to distract her, but I wanted to chuck my pizza crust at somebody's head. There they were, rattling away about how their garden was shaping up for fall, while my father was fighting for his life less than a hundred feet away.

Matthew tapped me on the leg, and said, "You know what's weird? When we were little, I always thought Dad was the strongest person on earth. Didn't you?"

I pictured swimming into his arms at the community center pool, and nodded.

"When he was teaching me how to throw a baseball, or how to catch, or how to hit—any of it—I just felt like he was Superman. Like he could do anything. And then one time, I was pitching baseballs to him in the backyard when I was eight or something, and I bounced one. It took a strange hop and came up right into Dad's, um, most sensitive area."

I wasn't sure where Matthew was going with this story. I wasn't sure I wanted to find out, either.

"So Dad basically keeled over to the right in slow motion. I ran over and shouted, 'Daddy, are you okay?' He was like, 'I'm fine, son. Just go inside the house. I'll be there in a little while.' I said, 'Should I get Mommy?' He looked up at me, and his jaw was clenched. He said, 'Just get in the freaking HOUSE!'"

I still didn't get it. "Soooo . . . you're saying . . . ?"

Matthew sighed. "Dad wouldn't have wanted us to see him looking like that, Claire. He must *hate* this."

I leaned my head on my brother's shoulder. On the other side of me, Grandma was asking Mom whether she had any good recipes for squash-and-apple casserole.

"Ahem," Dr. Venkersammy said. Somehow he had managed to maneuver himself within three feet of the whole family without anyone even noticing. He must have thought we were the least caring next of kin he had ever seen, babbling about baseballs and recipes while our loved one was ... was ... well, we didn't know what was going on at the moment.

"Doctor, is there news?" Mom asked.

He cleared his throat again. "Yes. In fact, I have good news and bad news. Which do you want first?"

9. A Really Rough Monday

If there were a nuclear holocaust, my mom would send me to school the next day. Everybody else would be hiding in their basements, sealed away with duct tape, eating canned peaches and beef jerky, but I'd be the one kid marching through the fallout past all the burned-out cars, the bodies, and the radioactive looters so I could be the only kid in jazz band.

Well, okay, Ryder would probably show up, too, just to spite me.

But, anyway, Mom sent Matthew and me to school on the Monday after the stroke because she said there was no use in our sitting around the hospital, moping. Matthew was so tired after spending most of the weekend watching a machine force air in and out of Dad's lungs that he just went along with everything Mom said, but I tried to argue a little bit, because I couldn't stand to leave my father's bedside. Mom just gave me a look I had never seen from her before, kind of like "Don't mess with me! My husband is in a medically induced coma!"

To be fair, how often does one get a chance to convey all that with a look?

So I went to school. I hadn't told anybody about the stroke. It seemed terrible to say it over social media or by text, and I was afraid I would cry if I said it out loud, so I'd just ignored several texts from my friends over the weekend. Every step of my walk felt like a mile. I was dreading having to deal with everyone's reactions to the news, but even more, I just kept worrying about what might happen to my father while I wasn't there. The doctor had said the first several days were the most dangerous time for stroke patients. Apparently, now that the original blood clot had dissolved, we still had to worry about another stroke, or pneumonia, or a heart attack, or bleeding ulcers, or a million other things. Dad could even get a bedsore and then die of an infection from *that*.

But sure, I was going to focus on polynomial factoring and whatnot.

At my locker, I was greeted warmly by the lovely Ryder, who said, "Hey, Goldsmith! Guess what? I just did my chair audition. I nailed all the mandatory major scales, some minors, some blues scales . . . I practiced all weekend. I know, I know . . . I'm awesome. You probably spent your weekend dancing or something, right?"

I stared at him and tried not to either (A) cry or (B) grab his throat and squeeze until his eyes popped out like champagne corks.

"So anyway, you might as well practice six or seven scales, because that's about right for your level. I just thought you'd want to be reminded of your sad, feeble place in the universe."

As soon as he scurried away to his locker like the loathsome vermin he was, Roshni appeared. "Hey," she said. "Your pimple cleared up!"

I touched my nose and realized that was true. Not that she had necessarily needed to announce it to the hallway at large.

"But why have you been ignoring my texts? Are you mad because I didn't yell at Ryder and Regina at lunch the other day? My parents always tell me I should be more forceful. Is that what it was? If it is, I'm sorry. I just get so flustered when people are angry and—"

"Roshni, it wasn't anything you did."

"Is your phone broken? I told you to convince your parents to get you a smartphone. They have the money. I don't know why they make you walk around with that cheap plastic—"

"Roshni, my phone works fine!"

"Then what is it?"

I bit my lip. Some things are just really hard to say. Like "I'm having my period." Or "Ryder actually is good at playing the sax." Or, evidently, "My father had a stroke and can't breathe on his own." I took a deep breath.

Regina walked up from behind me and said, "Hey, Goldsmith! I just heard about your father. That *sucks*."

Roshni said, "Oh my God! What happened to your dad?"

I stood there like a moron, trying to find the right words.

Regina didn't have the same problem. "Listen, I heard she was home with him, and all of a sudden, he just collapsed. And now he's in the hospital. They're saying it was a stroke."

Roshni said, "A stroke?"

Regina said, "Yeah. You know, when your brain goes, like, FWOOSH? My grampa died of that. It was ugly. Anyway, be nice to Starbuck today."

Roshni said, "Oh, Claire. Why didn't you tell me?" I was like, *I tried, but nobody around here knows how to shut up for twelve seconds.* Then she put her arms around me, and I kind of melted into her shoulder and closed my eyes. When I opened them again, Ryder was standing across the hall, looking like someone had just smacked him.

. . . .

In class, I kept thinking about what the doctor had said when he came out into the waiting room. First the good news: "Your husband's stroke was confined to a relatively small area of the brain, and the clot appears to be completely dissolved now." When I heard that, I'd thought, *Yay! He's going to be okay! A couple of weeks in the hospital, and then it will be back to normal! We're fine! Mom was right—never worry until you have to. We're going to be a-o—*

"And what small area of the brain are we talking about?" Mom had asked.

"Well, that's the bad news," the doctor had said, looking away for a moment. "There are two language centers located in the left side of the brain, and your husband's clot cut off the blood flow between them for several hours. Typically, in cases like this one, we expect to see, in addition to the usual weakness of the right side of the body, significant and ongoing difficulties with communication."

"But . . . but . . . my husband is a novelist!"

Dr. Venkersammy sighed. "I'm sorry, Mrs. Goldsmith. That is . . . most unfortunate. But please try to understand: I see stroke patients come in here almost every day. A significant percentage of them don't survive long enough

81

to get to the hospital, or have such severe brain swelling that they don't make it through the first day. Your husband's stroke may seem catastrophic in the context of your daily life, but it is not what we would categorize as a catastrophic stroke. Mr. Goldsmith will probably get to go home several days from now. He will be alive, breathing on his own, probably eating on his own, probably with some mobility."

Probably eating on his own? How was this not catastrophic?

"So. Your husband's outcomes should be on the milder end of the stroke spectrum if he works hard in therapy, and if he has a lot of support at home. He probably won't be doing any singing or dancing for a while, and his career situation is regrettable, but your husband is alive, and where there is life, there is hope."

Then some kind of social worker had come out to talk to Mom about setting up physical therapy for Dad, and I had sat down and cried. My dad without singing or dancing wasn't my dad at all.

. . . .

In the middle of history class, I got caught up in remembering a made-up song my father used to sing with us in the kitchen when we were little. Once, Mom had written *"butt. squash"* on the shopping list on the side of the refrigerator. Apparently, that stood for "butternut squash," but Matthew had read it out loud and started laughing. He'd asked what butt squash was, and Dad had burst into song:

> *"Butt squash, 1-2-3,*
> *Butt squash, you can look like me!*
> *Butt squash, down to the floor!*
> *Butt squash, just a little bit more!"*

And then the three of us had started doing a made-up dance that involved squashing ourselves down near the floor and wiggling our butts. When Mom walked into the kitchen, she had been all serious, like, "What? It says 'b-u-t-t period squash.' That's a perfectly logical abbreviation for 'butternut squash.'" And then one of us had shouted out "Butt squash!" and the song and dance started up again.

How could a man like that lose everything that made him *him?*

I asked if I could use the restroom, and spent the rest of the period walking randomly through the hallways. The teacher gave me a weird look when I came back at the end of class, but I just rubbed my stomach, and she nodded sympathetically.

At lunch, Roshni wanted to know everything. I didn't think I could get through all of it without bursting into hysterics, plus the cafeteria isn't exactly the most soothing or private spot, so I told her the absolute shortest version I could. Meanwhile, every few seconds, somebody new would come by and pat me on the shoulder and say, "I'm so sorry about your dad." I knew they were trying to be sweet and all, but it just made me feel even worse, like the whole lunchroom was staring at me. Even Christopher, the kid with autism, stood next to me, looked into the space just over my shoulder, and said, "I heard that your father had a stroke. Do not worry. Eighty percent of stroke patients survive their initial hospital stay. That's four out of five. The majority of stroke patients who make it to the hospital alive survive for at least one year."

Then he walked away. I was like, *Uh, thank you?*

Ryder and Regina sat at the other end of the table. I guess they were giving me a break. It wasn't like that solved all my problems or anything, but Roshni seemed to enjoy the extra Skittles.

In science, while I was supposed to be wiping up my desk after a measuring lab, I started thinking about another one of the songs my father used to make up, a catchy little number called "The Wiping Cloth." He would always sing it after dinner when he was doing the dishes. It went to the tune of "America," from the play *West Side Story*, although of course I hadn't known that when I was little. I closed my eyes and pictured him dancing and snapping that dish towel, belting out his imaginary Broadway showstopper:

> "I like to use-a the wiping cloth,
> I like to use it to wipe me off!
> I like to use-a the wiping cloth,
> I like to use it to wipe meeeeeeee off!"

Then Mrs. Selinsky yelled at me for daydreaming. One second, I was a happy little five-year-old in my kitchen with my daddy, and the next, some insane lady was spitting in my face from a foot away, shouting, "You know who always paid attention in class? *Meredith* always paid attention in class! Don't you want to be a Meredith, Clarabelle?"

I said, "Um, my name is Claire."

"Okay, Clara. Well, *do* you want to be a Meredith? I don't think you want it enough. Watch your step." Then she started walking backward away from me, and stumbled over the classroom trash can.

In the hallway, Roshni said to me, "Wow, that was kind of crazy, huh? I should have defended you, especially today. I'm sorry I didn't say anything. You know, one day, I *am* going to say something to that lady. I'm going to get right in her face and be all like, 'Nobody cares about your stupid daughter, so why don't you shut up about her and try actually teaching us some science for a change?' I swear, that woman is, like, brain damaged or something. Oh, God. I don't mean brain damaged. I'm sorry I said brain damaged. Claire, where are you going? I was just trying to stick up for you. Okay, I guess I'll text later to see how you're doing—"

As I walked around the corner and out of hearing range, she was still talking.

Before leaving school, I stopped by the band room to sign up for a chair audition slot. I put my name down for the earliest time before school on Thursday because I figured coming to school early would be easier than staying late, with everything that was happening with my father.

Ryder came out of the band room, holding his saxophone, and bumped into me. "Claire," he said, "I'm sorry I said all that stuff about the audition today. I didn't know your father was in the hospital, I swear."

"Oh, thanks, Ryder. So you're sorry you were mean to me because my father is in the hospital?"

"Well, yeah."

"But you're not sorry you've been mean to me every other day ever since we got to middle school? You've been all over me from the first week of sixth grade. Why should you change just because my dad's brain is swollen and he might never walk or talk right again? You know what? I don't want you to suddenly start being nice to me just because you pity me. Just keep being a jerk. After all, that's *about right for your level.*"

It felt great to shut Ryder up for once. He turned away and trudged off down the hall without another word. I watched until he turned a corner and disappeared.

Grandpa picked me up from school and drove me to the hospital. There was a tiny celebration going on, because the doctors had taken out Dad's oxygen tube that morning, and he was breathing well on his own. My mom said this was a great step, but at the same time, in a way, it was scarier to be in the room now. With the tube pumping his lungs, at least we had known he wouldn't stop breathing. Without the machine, it was possible.

In fact, according to Christopher, there was a one-in-five chance.

A few minutes after I walked in, Dad's mother arrived. Gram had been away on a cruise when he had the stroke and had come straight from the port in New York City to see her son. I knew she had been calling Mom on the phone a lot, and she had texted Matthew and me several times to see how we were doing. But when she got to the room, she went straight for Dad.

Well, first she dropped her huge purse in a chair. But then she leaned over his bed, wrapped both arms around him, and said, "Oh, Davey," in the most painful voice I've ever heard. He muttered something back that sounded like a question. She pulled back, and I saw that her eyes were all glossed over with tears. She grabbed both of his hands and said, "What was that, buddy?"

Which was so strange, because my dad always called me buddy when I was sad or hurt.

Dad just made a grunting sound, but Gram acted like it had made sense.

"That's right," she said. "I'm Mom. I'll be right back, okay? I just have to fix my makeup." At that point, my strong, take-charge grandmother, a college dean who had written two textbooks and survived two husbands, staggered out into the hallway. I heard an odd kind of yelping noise that I'd never heard before, and saw Matthew go out after her. I followed, and found my brother basically supporting my grandmother's weight as she sagged against him and wept hysterically. I didn't know what to do, so I walked around behind my brother and hugged her from the other side.

I wondered how long Matthew's arms would hold out, but before he collapsed and dropped her, Gram straightened up, wiped her eyes, cleared her throat, and said, "So, Claire, you were with him when this happened?"

I nodded.

"Oh, brave girl," she said, and grabbed me in some kind of Jewish-grandmother judo headlock. *Wow,* I thought, *nobody's ever called me brave before. Or choked me quite this hard.*

"I didn't really do anything, Gram. I just called 9-1-1."

"Darling. You saved your father's life. Whatever happens, don't you ever forget that. Now I just need to go find a bathroom and put my face back on."

As she walked away, Matthew made a little "humph" noise in the back of his throat and headed into the room. But I was like, *That's what I'm talkin' about. I'm a lifesaver, baby!*

For some reason, though, late that night, I couldn't stop thinking about what had happened between me and Ryder in the band hallway. I kept hearing his voice, apologizing, and my voice, telling him off. When I finally closed my eyes to sleep, all I could see was the wounded look in Ryder's eyes right before he turned and walked away.

10. Blowing It

That week may have been the longest of my life. Dad gradually became more alert, and started sitting up in bed on Tuesday. Oh, and vases of flowers, bunches of balloons, and edible fruit arrangements began filling up the room. On Wednesday, he began doing physical therapy exercises. He hadn't started using the right words for anything, though, and his whole right side was still droopy.

As for me, I worried my way through school, and then spent every waking minute of the evenings at the hospital, except when I had dance classes. I told my mom I could stay with Dad and miss dance, but she insisted that going to the classes was part of keeping my life "normal."

You know, because all the girls my age were commuting from the intensive care unit to fifth-grade ballet lessons. Looking back, I have to say that my grandparents were amazing, because they were the taxi service, the food service, and basically the life-support system for Matthew and me the whole time Dad was in the hospital for that first stretch. As it was happening, though, I wasn't grateful. I missed having my father in the driver's seat, cranking out Beatles songs on the stereo, singing outrageously loud harmonies, and making faces at the other drivers.

Grandma hates the Beatles.

And Mom was sleeping at the hospital, which meant we were sleeping at our grandparents' house, which was about a mile from ours. Every night when we got there after dance and I took my shower, I felt totally lonely because Mom had always brushed out my hair before bed. I wished she could be home with me, instead of in a chair next to Dad. I even thought, *She might as well be with me. What's the difference? It's not like he can really talk to her.*

And then I thought, *I am the worst person in the world.*

On Thursday morning, I woke up with a feeling of total doom in my stomach. I hadn't practiced for my chair audition at all. Ryder hadn't talked to me, or even looked at me, all week. He and Regina had stayed at the far end of the table at lunch every day. On the one hand, I was like, *Hey, Skittles!* But on the other, I was like, *What's his evil plan?* I was kind of hoping that wiping me out at auditions, and then watching me sink from second chair all the way down into the second or third row somewhere, might be enough to make him feel he had gotten his revenge for the way I'd yelled at him on Monday.

Even as I walked down the band hallway to play for Mrs. Jones, I kept waiting for him to pop out from behind a door to scare me or something. He didn't, though. In fact, I was the only kid in sight. It was like one of those eerie dreams where you're alone in school and then a murderer starts chasing you around, only this was much scarier, because it involved embarrassing myself in front of my section, the band, and my favorite teacher.

I mean, at least after you get butchered by some dude in a hockey mask, you don't have to listen to Ryder Scott following you around for six months, going, "Ha! You *so* got butchered by that dude in the hockey mask!" Although there's a pretty good chance he would show up at your grave and taunt you posthumously for a while.

Anyway, Mrs. Jones was waiting for me, score sheet in hand. "Claire, sweetheart, good morning! Did your family get the fruit basket the Band Parents' Association sent over?"

I nodded. It had basically been my dinner the night before. I was getting pretty sick of the hospital cafeteria food. "Yes, thank you."

"You know, we don't have to do this now if you don't want to. We could postpone it."

I shook my head.

"I wouldn't penalize you or anything." Mrs. Jones must

have incredibly bad eyes, because she wears huge, thick glasses that make it look like her pupils alone take up half her face. She was looking at me like the world's kindest barn owl.

"I know, but . . . it's okay. I'll play."

She patted me on the shoulder.

I took my saxophone out of its case, placed the audition music on the stand in front of me, tuned up quickly, and then froze completely. My legs were shaking. My heart was pounding so hard I could feel my pulse in my neck. I tried to calm down, I swear. I inhaled and exhaled three times to settle my nerves. But then I just sat there like a moron. I couldn't do this.

"Whenever you're ready, Claire."

I still sat. If I kept this up much longer, she was going to kick me out of the band, put a bucket of sand in the second chair, and just stick an alto sax in *that*.

"Do you need me to count you in?"

Nothing. Silence. Crickets.

"Claire. Honey. Are you sure you don't want to reschedule this?"

I turned to her and felt like my face was going to melt. "It's not about my dad, Mrs. Jones. I mean, it is—I didn't practice at all this week. I haven't even been in the same house with my horn. But—I don't know. I just can't . . ."

Mrs. Jones pushed her glasses all the way down her nose, peered over them at me, and said, "All right, this audition is officially over. I can't hear you at your best when your life is at its worst."

I sighed, and my pulse slowed. I felt like an invisible giant had just lifted his foot off the center of my chest.

"But you know, we have a few moments now before the school day begins. Would you like to run through the piece for me a couple of times?"

I played, and the first run-through was kind of choppy. The second one, though, was pretty good. I hit one fairly major wrong note near the end, but slurred up a half step into the correct note really fast, so the mistake wasn't so glaringly obvious.

As soon as I finished with that, Mrs. Jones whipped the sheet music away and said, "Now how about some scales, just for practice?"

I ran through the mandatory scales, plus a bunch of optional ones, and everything went smoothly. Somehow, playing music felt good. It was a lot like dancing; it's really hard to play and worry at the same time.

When I was done running the last scale, Mrs. Jones said, "You know, if that had been your real audition, you would have made fifth chair. I know that's a slight drop down, but it's not terrible, considering what's been going on in your life lately. I'd say if you can find the time to do some woodshedding this weekend, you can—"

"I'll take it!" I said.

"What?" she asked.

"If you'd be willing to count this as my real audition, I would take fifth chair. I mean, I appreciate your extension offer and everything, but it really wouldn't be fair to everyone else. And this way, I can just concentrate on being with my dad."

Mrs. Jones thought for a moment, and then smiled at me. "Oh, brave girl!" she exclaimed. "Welcome to fifth chair! I've never been so proud to demote somebody before." She pushed her glasses back up her nose, and I noticed her eyes were welling up with highly magnified tears.

I was sure I was going to get absolutely sandblasted by Ryder about this, but, hey—at least I had been called brave twice in a week. That was a personal record.

. . . .

I had a private lesson with the strictest teacher at the dance school, Miss Laura, that night. I asked her whether she thought it would be possible for me to get moved up into the higher classes with my friends. She said, "Honestly?"

I gulped. This was not a woman who was known for holding back. I couldn't imagine what her unfiltered, honest opinion would be like. But I really, really wanted to move up, so I said, "Honestly."

"Well. Your turns are slow. You need a bigger plié before your leaps. Your arms are like spaghetti, and you aren't graceful."

"And what's the bad news?"

If her eyebrows hadn't already been completely plucked out and redrawn in pencil, Miss Laura would have raised them and sneered at me. She's not a big humor fan. *All righty, then*, I thought. *All I have to do is change . . . everything. You know, get good. Stop sucking. Turn into Alanna. No big.* I stepped over to the barre and said, "Just kidding. Can we please get started?"

. . . .

On Friday, I found myself one-on-one with my father for the first time since his stroke. Gram had gone to New York for a couple of days to take care of some things, but was back again. Mom and Gram had gone out to a Chinese takeout place to pick up dinner, and Matthew was off playing in a soccer game. I had begged my mother not to leave me there alone because I was sort of afraid of my dad. I mean, the last time I'd been alone with him, he'd almost died. I told my mom this, and asked, "What am I supposed to do if he has another massive crisis?"

She said, "Just grab this remote control right here and push the big red call button. Now, have a nice conversation with your father. He loves you. Your voice is good for him."

Then she walked out. Like I wasn't already scarred for life enough.

I didn't know where to look, how to act, or what to say. Dad kept looking at me as if he wanted to tell me something important, so I got up from the chair I'd been sitting in and sat on the edge of his bed. But then he didn't say anything, so I decided that maybe I should just tell him about my week. Mom, Matthew, and everyone else in the family had been talking to him as though he could still understand, even though there wasn't any way to know. People had tried asking him all sorts of yes-or-no questions and getting him to nod or shake his head; sometimes the answers made sense, sometimes they didn't, and sometimes he just stared into space while completely ignoring the speaker.

I couldn't stand the silence, so I launched into a whole big speech—about Ryder and my audition and my dance issues. I told him how much I missed talking with him and how much I needed his advice. I even told him how sorry I was that we'd argued the night before the stroke.

Then I felt stupid, because if he didn't understand any of this, it was all completely pointless. I figured there was a fifty-fifty chance I might as well have been directing my monologue at the huge bundle of Clifford the Big Red Dog balloons Dad's publisher had sent over on Wednesday.

I couldn't take not knowing, so I squeezed Dad's hand and asked, "Dad, do you know what I'm saying? Do you know who I am?"

He stared at me for the longest, scariest time, and then said, "Piggy? Piggy! Piggy!"

I threw my arms around him and burst into tears. He *did* understand. He *did* know me. When I was little, I used to hide under my blankets when I didn't want to get up in the morning. My father would sit on the edge of my bed and say, "Where's my daughter? Where's Claire? I think she's gone! But there's some kind of lumpy thing under her covers! Let me just . . . poke . . . at . . . it . . . a bit and see what I can figure out."

Then he would poke and tickle me through the covers, "finding" my face, knees, feet, elbows, et cetera, but mistaking them for various animal parts. Sometimes, he would declare that I was a snake or an elephant or a deadly jungle cat. But most often, he would grab one of my elbows and pretend he thought it was a pig's snout. Then he would shout "PIGGY!" as he whipped the blankets off.

We called that game Playing Piggy.

When my mother and Gram came back with the food, I was trying to teach Dad to say my actual name. I would go into a whole, lengthy explanation, like, "Yes, Piggy is a game we used to play. But that's not my real name. My real name is Claire. Can you say 'Claire'?"

Then he would get all animated, lean forward, and yell, "Piggy!"

Mom and Gram thought this was great. Mom said that the doctors had told her Dad might not have the right names for things, but when he started naming things at all, it would be an important step.

So I worked on getting Dad to name the other people in the room. When it was my mom's turn, he didn't even come close to saying *Nicole*, but he did point to her and say, "Bug." She got all teary-eyed and told me that when they had first started dating, his mushy nickname for her was Herbie Love Bug. She had called him Pork Chop.

Which didn't sound that romantic, but whatever.

Next, I tried to get him to call his mother *Mom*. He kept looking away and bunching up a handful of bedcovers in his left fist, like this was a really frustrating assignment, but then he finally whipped his head around, made eye contact with Gram, and said, "Hat! Hat!" in a soft, little-kid voice.

Gram teared up, too, and said, "That was his first word. He used to crawl around the house all the time holding this little blue hat his aunt Iris had made him, and he would say it just like that—'Hat! Hat!'"

Dad smiled and said it again. His hand released its grip on his blankets, and he lay back and closed his eyes.

In probably less than a minute, he was snoring. Mom told us the doctors had said remembering would be exhausting work for him, and that we were supposed to let him sleep as much as he needed to.

We sat and ate our Chinese food in total silence. I kept remembering what it had been like, hiding under my blankets and waiting for Dad to "find" me. Even when I was, like, seven years old, a small part of me had sort of half believed he hadn't known it was me under there. Mom and Gram looked far away, too. I guess Mom was having dinner with her Pork Chop, and Gram was picturing her little boy crawling around with a blue hat.

I don't know how long we all would have sat there, but after fifteen minutes or so, Matthew burst into the room with Mom's parents right behind. "We won!" he shouted. "I scored my first varsity goal. Aw, Mom, it was beautiful. I was way out past the eighteen. There were two guys on me, but I juked and got the shot off—lefty! The keeper dove for it, but it bent around him and went in. Back upper ninety for the win! Oops, is Dad asleep?"

Our father sat up, looked right at my brother, and said, "Matthew!"

So typical.

11. At Home with Baby Dad

My favorite of my dad's books is called *Out of the Cradle*. The title comes from a poem by his favorite poet, Walt Whitman. Anyway, the last line of the novel goes, "And that's how we live: wandering endlessly, concentrically outward, seeking in others a kindling spark of the love which has long lain dormant, dark, unstoked in our own deepest souls."

On the morning of his discharge from the hospital, I kept thinking of that sentence over and over, wondering whether he would ever write anything like that again. Write it? I was wondering whether he'd ever even be able to *understand* anything like that again. A parade of professionals came into the room and went over the discharge instructions with Mom—which was an endless recital of "He *can* eat this; he *can't* eat that; he *might* be able to eat this other thing, but only on Fridays when the moon is three-quarters full" and "He's walking *great*—well, not great in the sense of being able to walk more than fifteen feet without a cane, or being able to handle stairs, or having good balance, but, hey, he's walking and that's great!" and "You have to give him this medicine twice a day with food, this medicine three times a day without food, but with plenty of liquid, and this medicine four times a day with food, liquid, a spoonful of sugar, and the blessings of three monks from a cave in the Himalayas." Mom looked so overwhelmed I thought she might just pass out.

Who could possibly keep all this stuff straight?

. . . .

And then my father came home. Gram waited at the house to help on that end, while Mom, Matthew, and I all escorted him out of the hospital and into our minivan. The whole way, I felt tremendously panicked. I was like, *Help! Don't send him home with us! We don't know what we're doing! Here he has doctors, nurses, nutritionists, physical therapists, speech therapists, occupational therapists, breathing therapists—I'm pretty sure his therapists have therapists. At home he'll have a bunch of total amateurs. I can't even keep a goldfish alive. Matthew once bought a hamster and didn't notice for three days that it had escaped. Three freaking days! Do you know how far our father could get in three days?*

Possibly all the way to the front door.

Anyway, it took a big male nurse-dude and Matthew to help Dad into the front seat of the minivan, and I was like, *Do you people think we have a guy like that just randomly standing in our driveway, waiting to drag my father out of the car? What are we supposed to do, call 1-800-LIFT-POP?*

I hadn't really thought it through, but our whole life was going to get flipped over and shaken around. I mean, the hospital was one thing, but once he got home, this was *the rest of our lives.*

Matthew and Gram got Dad into our family room through the garage, because that was the only entrance that didn't involve stairs. That was another thing: Our house was a minefield of staircases. First, you had the family room and a half bath on the garage level, with stairs down to the basement from there. You had to walk up five steps from the family room to reach the kitchen, living room, and dining room, and another seven to get to the bedrooms and the main bathroom.

What were we supposed to do, crank Dad up and down using pulleys? Was he going to live on the family room couch? There wasn't even a shower in the bathroom on that level.

I also had two really selfish thoughts. First of all, what was I going to say when my friends came over and found my unshowered, dirty father lying on the pullout couch all day, drooling, barking nonsense words, and referring to me as Piggy? And second, the family room was where I did all my stretching and core exercises for dance, because I liked the carpeting there. Where was I supposed to work out if Dad was permanently camping on the sofa?

"We're home, honey!" Mom said in a fake-cheerful voice.

"Waldron!" Dad replied.

"What the heck is a Waldron?" Matthew asked.

"It's the street he grew up on in New York," Gram said. It was so strange: Everything Dad said made a weird kind of sense, but only if you knew enough about his life to skip a step along with him. Was that just how things were going to be forever?

"Spicy!" Dad said.

"Our cat when he was a little boy," Gram said.

"Jesus Christ!" Mom said, and leaned her head against the wall. "How are we going to get through this?"

My mom and Gram hadn't ever been close—I mean, they were in-laws—but Gram put her hands on Mom's shoulders and said, "You'll do it the same way you've always done everything, Nicole: extremely well."

Holy cow. That was the nicest thing either of my grandmothers had ever said to her kid-in-law. It was a total *moment*, until I noticed something: Our whole house had been messed up. There were grippy railings leading around the edge of the family room to the bathroom, and then to the stairs. Somehow in the couple of days since I had last been home, the whole place had been worked over.

I felt like the bears in Goldilocks: *Someone's been sleeping in my bed, and they've brought power tools!*

I ran upstairs, and there was a railing installed to connect the downstairs stair banister to the one that led to the bedrooms, and another that ran the whole length of the upstairs hallway, into the bathroom, and then into my parents' bedroom. My bedroom was unchanged—which was kind of a relief, because for a moment, I had been afraid it might have been turned into some kind of therapy pool for Dad or something—but the bathrooms were both bizarrely altered. The downstairs one had a weird, tall thing strapped on top of the toilet to make the seat higher, and guardrails on either side. The upstairs one had a railing on the shower wall, plus a plastic-and-metal seat actually in the tub itself. I examined the seat and saw that it could fold up and out of the way for when the rest of us were using the shower, but still—our entire home was like a gigantic hospital room.

I ran back down to the family room, where Matthew was already looking outraged. "Mom," I said.

"This is not the time, Claire. I just told your brother the same thing. Now go to your room and study or something until dinner."

"But—but—I don't have anything to study. And it's only two o'clock."

Mom rubbed her right temple with two fingers, which she only ever does when her head hurts. "Just find something to do with yourself. Or I will find something for you. Is that clear?"

Matthew and I both got out of there so fast that if we had been in a cartoon, you would have seen colored blurs, and possibly trails of smoke, behind us.

Mom made Dad's favorite dinner, spaghetti and meatballs. Unfortunately, if you have ever seen a toddler try to eat spaghetti, you will realize she hadn't really thought that one all the way through. It was a massacre. The doctors said Dad's recovery of his swallowing reflex had been amazing, because apparently, after a stroke, lots of people can't eat or drink much without either choking or inhaling the food into their lungs.

But you can't swallow the food if you can't get it into your mouth, and Dad had been right-handed before the stroke. Now his right hand was kind of weak, curled, and spastic. He was trying to do everything with his left, but if you try to do something like get spaghetti onto a fork and to your mouth with your bad hand, you will be surprised by how challenging it is. And *you* haven't had a stroke, which messes up things like balance and body awareness, too.

107

What I am saying is that Dad was essentially trying to catapult the food at his face in the hope that some would go in. As a result, his face looked like a thirteenth-century French castle under attack. We all tried to ignore this for a while, but finally Mom said, "Here, can I help you with that?"

He just stared straight ahead, as if he hadn't heard, and chucked a meatball over his shoulder into the white lace curtains.

Mom wiggled the sauce-covered fork out of his hand, speared a tiny piece of meatball from his plate, and brought it to his lips, but he didn't do anything.

"Bite, Dad," I said, but he just stared at the wall.

"Open?" Mom asked, but he still stared.

Then Mom asked Matthew to help her turn Dad's chair, and they got Dad positioned so that he was facing her on an angle. Next, she took a bit of food onto her own fork and put that down on her plate while easing Dad's fork back into his hand.

I found myself holding my breath as she slowly brought her fork up. Dad slowly lifted his, too. She opened her mouth, and after a few seconds' delay, Dad opened his. She brought her fork to her lips, and Dad did the same, but his fork was off course. Matthew jumped up and guided Dad's arm a bit until everything was lined up.

I could barely stand to watch.

Mom put her food into her mouth, closed, and chewed.

Dad's fork went in. He closed his mouth, a bit crookedly, and chewed. Only a little bit of sauce dribbled out.

When she swallowed, Dad swallowed. When she opened her mouth and smiled, so did he.

Then Dad tried to take another forkful of spaghetti, but he couldn't seem to find his plate with the fork. He just kept stabbing the table instead. Matthew tried to guide his arm, but Dad shrugged him off with a glare. After five or six stabs, Dad dropped his fork, shoved a hand into his spaghetti, grabbed a hunk, and shoved it into his mouth.

Mostly.

"Oh, honey!" Mom said.

"Meat! Me eat!" said the great author.

12. Some Harmless Cannibal Humor

When Matthew was in the eighth grade, he was president of the jazz band. He was the only kid in his entire year to have straight A's through all three years of middle school. He was the star shortstop of his travel baseball team, and captain of his travel soccer team. When he walked through the halls of the school, lesser students waved palm fronds to cool his skin and dropped aromatic petals in front of his feet.

Okay, that last part isn't true. As far as I know.

But you can see why I might have felt insecure about my place in the world, especially when my semi-vegetative father started calling me Piggy but still remembered Matthew's name every time. Plus, I was now fifth chair in band and had been demoted to Baby's First Dance Class.

I decided I needed to do something fun, different, and flashy to cheer myself up. Obviously, my two-hundred-dollar boots hadn't exactly blown anybody away, so fashion wasn't going to do the trick for me. But right after Dad came home, my history teacher, Mr. Evans, assigned us a project on any aspect of American history up through the Revolutionary War. Now, you have to understand, Mr. Evans had a sick sense of humor. So I figured I could go a little crazy with my presentation.

I decided to go with a "Miserable Deaths of the Explorers" theme. This stuff was awesome material. Henry Hudson was marooned with his son and a few faithful companions to freeze and die in a rowboat in an icy bay—picture the end of *Titanic*, but without the sexy parts. Captain James Cook was clubbed and stabbed to death by angry Hawaiians. Giovanni da Verrazano went ashore on a tropical island in a small boat with a few men, and was then killed and eaten by cannibals in the Caribbean while the rest of his crew watched helplessly from their ship. Juan Rodríguez Cabrillo jumped down from his ship onto some rocks to help his crew when they were attacked by natives, but broke either an arm or a leg when he landed. The limb got infected, and he died several days later. Ferdinand Magellan was hacked to death by Pacific Islanders with spears and blades. But my all-time favorite was probably Juan Ponce de León, who got shot in the leg with a poisoned arrow in Florida.

First, I considered doing Explorer Death Charades. Unfortunately, when I tried the game out with Roshni, it turned out to be impossible to tell the difference between Magellan and Cook, because getting slaughtered in hand-to-hand combat in Hawaii looks a lot like getting slaughtered in hand-to-hand combat on any other island. Also, the Verrazano part was tricky, because by the time I got around to him, I was an expert at getting killed by natives, but "eaten while his crew watched helplessly" was beyond my technical miming abilities.

On the bright side, if I ever need to pretend I am getting shot with a poisoned arrow, jumping from a height and mangling myself, or freezing to death in slow motion while rowing a boat, I have those *down*.

I chucked the mime idea and switched over to a poster project, which was much easier. I drew each explorer's death scene on one side of the paper, with the explorers' names listed out of order on the other. Whoever looked at the poster could try to match up each death with the right explorer.

That took me two entire evenings, which, combined with my scheduled dance nights, meant I got to avoid a whole week of family dinner ordeals. When it was done, I was pretty pleased with myself. I couldn't imagine anybody else had spent this much effort on their project.

During the coloring phase, I used a *lot* of red marker.

When I was completely finished with the poster, my mother asked me whether I wanted to go with her, Dad, and Matthew to some kind of special therapy store to buy "mealtime adaptive items" for the house. I was like, *I'd rather just stay here and get Verrazano'd by enraged, hungry islanders.* Which gave me an idea: What if I also recorded a song to go with the poster? I asked Mom if I could stay home to work on my history project, and of course she had to say yes.

We had done a whole unit on song recording in seventh-grade music class, so I knew how to set up a background with instruments and stuff in a recording-software program on my laptop. It took only a few minutes to create a basic Caribbean-sounding tune. The words took me several hours, but at the end, I thought it came out pretty well:

> *I am having an awful day*
> *(Henry Hudson! Henry Hudson!)*
> *'Cause I'm freezing my butt to death on the bay!*
> *(Henry Hudson! Henry Hudson!)*
>
> *I thought Hawaii was pretty fab*
> *(Captain James Cook! Captain James Cook!)*
> *'Til I started gettin' clubbed and stabbed!*
> *(Captain James Cook! Captain James Cook!)*
>
> *Sometimes I just want to cry and beg*
> *(Juan Cabrillo! Juan Cabrillo!)*

'Cause I fell and died of a broken leg!
(Juan Cabrillo! Juan Cabrillo!)

You get the point. (So did Ponce de León.)

I saved the song to a flash drive, rolled up my poster, and headed off happily to school the next morning for the first time in weeks. I was totally right that nobody else had put nearly as much flair into the assignment as I had. Other people had boring charts like "Nutrition at the First Thanksgiving" or unoriginal essays or—in the most pathetic case—a macaroni sculpture of George Washington crossing the Delaware.

I was like, *Now, if he had been boiled while crossing the Delaware until he was al dente, that would be interesting.*

Ryder performed a "patriotic saxophone tribute to America," which was (A) completely off topic because there was nothing to be patriotic about until after the Revolution, and (B) the lamest example of a history project ever, because it didn't display any knowledge of history. As far as I could tell from Mr. Evans's reaction, Ryder's grade was a raised eyebrow.

Roshni's project was as morbid as mine. She had a whole PowerPoint on how European settlers had spread fatal diseases to the indigenous people. She spent the last few slides illustrating the dangers of smallpox-infected blankets. Then she turned off the projector, but before Mr. Evans could turn the lights on, she threw a blanket over the three kids in the middle of the front row: Christopher, Ryder, and Leigh. Ryder laughed, Christopher yelled, "Help! Smallpox!" and Leigh screeched, "My haaaiiiirrrr!"

Regina's project was a bunch of pencil drawings of famous Latino Americans, done on regular old loose-leaf paper. Some of the papers were crumpled, and there appeared to be stains on one or two pages. I had to admit the art was kind of amazing, though. At the beginning of the second day of presentations, we had time to walk around and look at all the silent projects. I spent a long time looking at one particular picture Regina had done. It was supposed to be some guy I had never heard of named Cesar Chavez. There was a quote from him under the drawing: "We draw our strength from the very despair in which we have been forced to live. We shall endure."

The thought made me think about my father. Was he going to draw strength from having his brain suddenly ruined for no reason? How could he draw strength when he couldn't even think?

Regina caught me looking at her work, and said, "What?"

I asked, "Is this a relative of yours?"

She said, "Are you kidding me? Just because we have the same last name, you mean? There are probably a million people in the world named Chavez. Cesar wasn't my relative. He was only the greatest labor leader this country has ever had. But of course you haven't learned about him in school, because he's not *important* enough."

I said, "God, Regina. I was just thinking—"

"What, that I used ghetto paper? Well, excuse me if there aren't any really fine craft stores within walking distance of my house, and my mom works late every night. I don't want to hear it, Starbuck."

"Uh, I was going to say I think you're a great artist."

Regina looked at me for the longest time without saying a word, like she wasn't sure whether I was serious.

When I played the recording of my song for the class, everybody seemed to like it. Some people laughed, and others were tapping along or bobbing their heads to the beat by the end. Even Mr. Evans chuckled.

Before I knew it, miserable explorer deaths became kind of a thing in my class.

Some kid slipped and fell down, like, half a flight of stairs, and one of the boys behind him said, "Whoa! Cabrillo alert!" At lunch, on meat loaf day, Regina bit into the mystery meat, and said, "Holy Verrazano, what am I eating? Quick, pass me some Skittles!" In flag football, when a whole bunch of kids attacked one person, that was the "Captain Cook play."

Then it was time for our once-a-year swimming rotation in gym. Everyone freaking hates swim-gym days, for about a million reasons. For one thing, the custodians are not professional pool maintenance people, so the pool is always either vaguely coated with a thin, green slime or so incredibly overtreated with chlorine that, after you swim in it, your hair has the consistency of straw for a month. For another thing, uh . . . it's eighth grade. You've got these obnoxious popular girls like Leigh Monahan with their perfect bodies, who probably schedule three weeks of tanning sessions when they know swimming is coming up, just so the boys will drool over them even more. But you've also got a few unlucky, teensy-weensy girls who look like they belong in my dance classes, some overweight girls who mostly come unprepared every day, stand around hunching over, with their arms crossed to cover every bit of themselves they possibly can, and then the main mass of basically-normal-but-self-conscious girls like me. I usually wear a tankini with boy-short bottoms that scream, *Hide my legs!* Meanwhile, Roshni sports some kind of ridiculous skirted suit in an attempt to conceal the fact that she has a butt. Jennifer's suit has weird poofy fringes that are supposed to camouflage ... well, I'm not sure what they're supposed to do. They mostly just make it look like she's wearing some kind of inflatable child flotation vest.

Not a flattering look, BTW.

So the girls are all wishing invisibility cloaks were a real thing. The boys are huddled in their own little groups, and it's the same ugly situation over there. You've got maybe three male Leigh types with actual six-packs and such, but the rest of the boys are either generally tiny, generally chubby, or sporting the made-from-mismatched-parts look.

So yeah, the first day of gym was a tense and horrifying scene. And then some friend of Ryder's walked by on the other side of the pool, and Ryder yelled, "HELP! I'm getting Verrazano'd!" Which was hilarious because, you know, they were across the water from each other and all.

Unfortunately, as soon as "Help!" left Ryder's mouth, the high school girl who was our official lifeguard jumped up, knocked over the table she was sitting at, which sent her books, her backpack, and the school's official swimming time clock skittering across the tiles into the pool, and shouted, "WHERE?"

She was a little jumpy. I guess it was probably her first day, too.

The gym teacher, Mr. Banyon, went nuts. First, he got right into Ryder's face and screamed, "Why are you shouting 'Help!' in a crowded pool?"

Ryder said, "Um, I wasn't in the pool, sir. I was next to the pool."

"But when you shout 'Help!' it creates a dangerous situation. The lifeguard thought you were actually in the water."

I think Ryder would have shut up then, but unfortunately, Christopher involved himself. "Mr. Banyon," he said, "Ryder said he was being Verrazano'd. Verrazano died on land, so Ryder could not have been in the water."

"What in the world are you talking about, Marsh?" barked the gym teacher. Because, you know . . . gym teacher.

"Verrazano didn't drown, he was eaten by cannibals while his crew watched from across a body of water. That is the analogy I believe Ryder was making. Now, if he had said, 'Help! I am being Henry Hudsoned!' that might have made more sense, because Henry Hudson was last seen alive on a small rowboat in dangerous, freezing waters, and may very well have drowned. But even then, we don't really know exactly how—"

"Are you people insane?" asked Mr. Banyon as the lifeguard girl grabbed the rescue pole-and-net thing off the wall and attempted to fish her binder and calculator out of the pool with it.

The yelling continued for so long that we never did get into the pool. So, hey, thanks, Juan Cabrillo.

But at the end of the day, Ryder cornered me at the lockers. "Thanks for getting me in trouble today in gym, Claire!" he barked.

"Me? What did I do?"

"You're the one who started all the stupid Cabrillo jokes!"

"Are you kidding me? You're the idiot who yelled 'Help!' at a crowded pool, genius. All I did was sit back with some popcorn and watch the show."

"I'm an idiot? *I'm* an idiot?"

"Well, yeah. I mean, I think you should say it with more of a sentence-like inflection, but you're definitely starting to get the idea."

Ryder and I were about three inches apart, shouting in each other's faces, when Regina walked by and said, "Dang, y'all *have* to work on your flirting skills. Because this is just pathetic."

At that moment, I was like, *Please Cabrillo me.*

13. They're Only Braces

Life at home was pretty weird. Dad basically just sat in the family room all day and watched TV, which didn't seem like it would be that much fun if you couldn't follow what people were saying. He had therapists and a visiting nurse, plus exercises to do on his own, but it still seemed like an amazingly dull existence. A few times, some of my parents' closest friends asked whether they could visit, but my mom kept putting them off. I heard her tell Grandma she didn't think my father would want anyone to see him so helpless. I kind of agreed with her.

Some of my friends complained that their dads were boring, but my dad had always been a fun person, you know? I hated seeing him plopped there on the couch with his remote control in one hand, and his stupid little finger-exercise squeezy balls in the other. He was supposed to be singing the wiping-cloth song, dancing around the kitchen, making everybody laugh.

It wasn't right. Neither was my response, which was to avoid being around him. I know it's stupid, but for a while in October and November, I almost pretended the guy on that couch was a stranger instead of my father. It was less painful that way. I wasn't sure how much he was aware of it, but clearly my mother and Matthew were. It took me a while longer to find out how much my absence was bothering my brother—partly because I was doing such a great job of avoiding everyone, and partly because Matthew and I hadn't been big on talking to each other, anyway—but Mom got on me immediately. She kept saying things like "While you're making excuses, everybody else is making time for Daddy. I mean, look at what Matthew has been doing. He—"

But I didn't want to hear about perfect Matthew. Plus, I really did have a lot to do. There was homework, or I had to go to the basement and practice dance, or I had yet another poster project, each one more elaborate than the one before. Everyone else's family tree for French class was just a plain old diagram on tagboard; mine was a three-dimensional Eiffel Tower made of toothpicks, with photos and descriptions of all my relatives hanging from it. For my father, I wrote "*Calme.*" That means "quiet," which had been the furthest thing from the truth until his stroke. But none of the words that had described him before were true anymore.

One day, Grandpa picked me up before school to take me for a regularly scheduled orthodontist appointment.

I had been going to these three times a year since the sixth grade. Every time, it was the same. The doctor would look at my latest X-rays, glance into my mouth, and say, "Not yet. Still waiting on a few more teeth to drop into place." Then he'd send me off to school.

But all of a sudden at this appointment, right after he looked at my teeth, the orthodontist snapped a big lamp thingy onto his forehead and turned on the light. I was like, *Is this guy planning to go mining for diamonds in my throat or what?*

"Today's the day, princess," he said.

An hour and a half later, I had a very sore jaw, several holes in my cheek where a wire had stabbed me, and my very own set of shiny braces. The joy was nearly overwhelming.

In a "Cabrillo me" kind of way.

I had been allowed to choose the colors for the little rubber brackets that went around the brace part on each tooth, and had gone with an alternating scheme of two blue teeth, two purple teeth. I thought the blue and purple would look nice with my blue eyes. My mom, Matthew, and I all have blue eyes. Dad always said that Mom's blue eyes were the first thing he noticed about her.

Anyway, when the dental assistant lady showed me my teeth in her handheld mirror, I thought the colors looked really good. I even texted Roshni, Jennifer, and Desi to tell them I had gotten braces and that I liked the way they looked. But when I got to school, Roshni was absent, and Jennifer and Desi apparently didn't agree with my assessment.

Jennifer said, "Ooh, let me see the new hardware!"

I smiled widely, thinking she would say something kind. You know, like any semi-decent human being might. Instead, she said, "Huh. So those are the colors you went with?"

Then Desi put her hands on my shoulders, physically turned me, stared into my mouth as though she was studying for a quiz on tonsil anatomy, and finally said, "Oh. Interesting choice."

I asked, "What do you mean, interesting choice? You can't just say 'interesting choice.' What's *that*?"

Desi let out an insincere little chuckle and said, "Well, don't you think blue is kind of, um, a *boy color*?"

Before I could respond, Jennifer said, "And purple is just kind of dark. We really think you should have minimized all that metal with something lighter. Like maybe white?"

"Or yellow?"

"Or even pink? You know? Because at least pink is feminine?"

I said, "I can't believe this. I got blue because my eyes are blue. And purple because I wear a lot of purple. Plus, why are you guys being so *mean*?"

Desi started tapping one foot, turned to Jennifer, and said, "See? I told you we shouldn't tell her our real opinions. I *knew* she was going to be like this."

Jennifer made a point of staring down at her nails and said, "Whatever. She asked us what we thought. It's not our fault if she picked weird colors."

I couldn't stand it. I turned to storm away and crashed right into Leigh Monahan. Leigh said, "HEY! Watch where you're—Oh, look! You got braces . . . *blue* braces."

I had already missed two classes, but the remainder of the morning was just like that. I felt like a freak show. Everybody kept coming up to me and checking out my teeth. Most people didn't say anything about the braces, but they didn't have to. Once Leigh Monahan had spoken, the grade had spoken. Unfortunately, unlike boots, braces were not an item that could be left at home.

Lunch was the worst. Without Roshni, I had no protection. Ryder and Regina didn't say anything about the braces, though. Instead, Ryder just went through the snack line and ordered a pile of things he knew I wouldn't be able to eat. Then he combined that with his usual hoard of junk food and offered me each item, gleefully.

The worst part was that I hadn't known I was going to get braces when I'd packed my lunch, so I had a brown bag full of stuff I couldn't chew: hard cheese with crackers, carrots, an apple, crunchy peanut brittle, and Skittles. Essentially, I had packed myself a lunch of rocks, diamonds, sticks, and bullets. And I was hungry. I popped half of a cracker in my mouth, hoping that if I just sucked on it long enough, it would sort of fall apart.

Meanwhile, I had to deal with Ryder waving Snickers bars, popcorn, baked Doritos, three kinds of gum, and hard candies under my nose.

Regina grinned at me and said, "You know you might as well just give me those Skittles, right?"

I pushed them across the table and ran out of the cafeteria, trying not to cry in front of everybody. I headed for the band room and got to sit there alone for a few minutes and calm down ... until three sixth-grade alto saxes came in together for a group lesson with Mrs. Jones. I tried to smile at them, and one of them, an awkwardly tall, red-haired girl whose name I could never remember, said, "Hey, I like your braces!"

That was when I finally broke down.

Mrs. Jones gave the sixth graders some warm-up scales, took me into her office, and hugged me. "Oh, kitten, are you having a bad day?" she asked.

No, I thought, *I'm having an early freaking Christmas. See the tinsel on my teeth?*

"You know, Claire, it's perfectly normal if you're depressed after what's been happening with your father and everything. Would you like me to call over to the guidance office and see whether the eighth-grade counselor is free?"

I forced myself to breathe deeply, and then said, "I'm not depressed. I'm just mad."

"Really? Why? You're usually so even-tempered."

Even-tempered? I thought. *How little you know me.* But of course I didn't say that. Instead, I mumbled, "Some people were making fun of my braces. I know, it's stupid."

"Honey," she said, "listen. When I was in eighth grade, my parents got divorced. For months, I felt like I was walking around on spiderwebs, like the slightest wrong step would make everything fall apart. And then one day in math class, a girl made fun of my jeans and I completely lost it."

Well, this was intriguing. "You lost it? What did you do?"

"I jumped up out of my seat, slapped her across the face in both directions, and then pushed my desk into the back of her chair so hard that she fell on the floor."

I couldn't help it. I laughed. "You . . . did *that?*" I gasped.

She smiled. "Yes, I did. And can I tell you a secret?"

I nodded.

"It felt . . . *excellent.*"

Right after she said this, Mrs. Jones seemed to suddenly remember she was a teacher, because she added, "But pretend you didn't hear that, all right? The important thing is that I know what it feels like when things aren't going right at home. And I'm here for you."

"Thank you," I said, and meant it. The mental picture of Mrs. Jones smacking the heck out of some 1980s mean girl had totally cheered me up. "And I'm not depressed. I promise. They're only braces, right?"

"Right," Mrs. Jones said.

. . . .

When I got home from school, Mom and Matthew were both helping Dad come out of the bathroom and walk up the stairs to the kitchen table. I smiled hugely at them, hoping they would notice my braces and say something nice, but they barely looked away from what they were doing. I sat there and watched Dad use one of his new, fat-handled spoons to eat some applesauce from one of his new bowls that attached to his new plastic table mat with suction cups, while Matthew made fake-cheerful small talk about his school day, and Mom worked on getting dinner into the oven.

And I smiled.

And smiled.

Matthew barely looked at me until Dad said, "Shiny Piggy!"

Both Matthew and Mom stopped and stared. Mom said, "Oh, Claire, I'd totally forgotten you were getting braces today! You look so cute!"

"Uh, yeah, Claire," Matthew said. "Those look nice on you."

Instead of making me feel good, this made me furious. "Mom," I snarled, "you *knew* I was getting my braces on today?"

"Well, sure, it's been on the calendar for a while."

"Why didn't you tell me?"

"I assumed you knew, Claire. And, well, we've all been kind of busy here."

"But I brought all the wrong stuff for lunch. I couldn't eat any of it. All I've had to eat all day is half a cracker. And everybody hated my braces! They laughed at me! This was the worst day of my life!"

"*This* was the worst day of your life, Claire?"

I said, "Yes. It was."

· "Really? After everything we've been through over the past month and a half? I want you to think really hard before you answer."

I looked around at my mom, who looked like she wanted to strangle me; at my brother, who looked kind of horrified; and finally at my father, who just sat there with applesauce dribbling down his chin, looking confused. Then I stood and went upstairs to my room.

I felt like I had just been Cabrillo'd, Captain Cooked, and then Henry Hudsoned. Actually, no. Henry Hudson had had a few faithful crew members in his little boat. I was sinking slowly in mine, all alone.

14. The Oblivious Dance

For the longest time, I didn't tell anybody in my dance world about Dad's stroke. I wasn't even sure how kids at school had found out so fast, but dance was my safe place, and I did not want to talk about brain injuries, blood clots, canes, walkers, or anything else there.

I managed to get away with it until a break between classes one night, when Katherine suddenly asked me, "What's your dad working on now?" The problem with having a father who writes books for teens is that everybody I know has read his work in school. It's the most bizarre thing ever. I remember when it first started happening to Matthew's friends. Kids who had known our father as a car-pool dad since preschool suddenly got all shy and giggly around him for, like, a week or two, and then got over it. I thought it was hilarious at the time . . . but it was much less amusing when it was *my* friends going through the weird phase.

Girls would come up to me at dance and be like, "I'm studying your *dad*. I had to read his website bio in class today. Did you know he dedicated his first novel to his son, Matthew, and his daughter, Claire?"

And I'd just be standing there, like, *If I had to stalk your parents for homework, do you think I'd march up to you and tell you about it?*

The one thing that every single person in the world seems to know about authors is that you're supposed to ask what they're working on. I don't know why. Katherine's dad is a surgeon, and I don't go up to her and ask if he's sliced up any interesting intestines lately.

Still, there she was in front of me, waiting for an answer. And what was I supposed to say—*He's working on identifying his family members? His meatball-splatter imagery is looking like a real artistic breakthrough? His newest project is bladder control?*

I just said, "Umm . . . he's kind of between books right now." Which was true, due to his inability to utilize the English language.

Katherine said, "Your dad is so nice. Remember when we first met at play rehearsal?"

Of course I did. It had been during fifth grade, at a community theater production of *Annie*. My father had been one of the volunteer scenery painters.

"And your father told you to crawl under the big desk of the orphanage right before dress rehearsal, and then look up? So you did, and he had painted *Claire rules!* on the bottom of the desk drawer? That was awesome."

I nodded. I had actually forgotten about that part.

"And this year, he's going to be onstage *with* you!"

I must have been staring at her as if she had two noses or something, because she added, "You know—for the father-daughter dance?"

My lips felt like they were made of lead as I said, "Yeah . . . right. Of course. I can't wait."

Alanna appeared then, sipping bottled water and smiling hugely. "The father-daughter dance. How *amazing* is that going to be? My dad is already getting nervous. Every week he's like, 'Do you know the theme yet? Is there music yet? Should we be practicing?' And I'm like, 'You're a dork!' But it's cute. Kind of. Oh, by the way—are your parents coming to the Halloween party this year?"

Oh, this is simply craptastic, I thought. Alanna's parents always threw a big Halloween party, and then Katherine, Alanna, and I would go over to Katherine's house for a sleepover. My mom made it to the party every year, and my father had probably gone to a couple of them.

If Mom didn't go to the party, she would mention Dad's stroke to Alanna's mom on the phone when she RSVP'd. And if Mom *did* go, she would tell everyone about the stroke during the party. If she somehow managed to haul Dad there—well, that was just too preposterous to contemplate.

Everybody at dance would stop thinking my father was awesome, and start knowing he was a broken shadow of his former self.

"Uh, I'm not sure. Can I get back to you on that?"

"No problem. Hey, Katherine, let's get back in the studio. I want to work on my fouettés before class starts up again. I need to be able to land four in a row cleanly. See you later, Claire."

Four fouettés? Nobody in my classes except me could even do one. A fouetté is the fast, spinning turn that dance schools always have the girls do together in performance in order to make the audience clap like crazy, but nobody ever claps until at least the third rotation. Which meant that there would be no spontaneous outbreaks of applause during any of my recital dances. Some of the girls in my group had about as much chance of landing a fouetté as my dad did.

The teachers would be better off just choreographing a triple Cabrillo. The injury rate would probably be roughly the same.

. . . .

I evaded Alanna's questions about the party until the week before Halloween, when I couldn't get out of dealing with the issue anymore. Then I had an idea: I would ask Matthew what he'd been telling his friends about our father.

He was sitting at the kitchen table doing homework, but I noticed he kept peeking past me at Dad, who was watching TV downstairs.

"You're kidding, right?" Matthew asked.

"No. Why would I be kidding?"

"Are you really that oblivious, Claire?" he said. I had never heard him sound so bitter before. I mean, he was a big brother, so of course he knew how to put me down. But not like this.

"What are you talking about?"

"Well, Claire Bear, my soccer team figured out there was something going on when I quit playing in the middle of the season so I could rush home every day to spend time with your father while your mother makes his dinner. My band friends noticed when I quit being section leader. My girlfriend noticed when *I broke up with her* so I would be here all night, every night, and all weekend. And I'm pretty sure everyone else got the memo when I stopped getting straight A-pluses for the first time in my life and dropped two of my AP classes. Does that answer your question?"

I sat down across from Matthew. It felt like someone had cut the tendons behind my knees. He was right. I was the most clueless person in the world. How had I not noticed that he was home around the clock? Sports were his life—I would have to have been the biggest moron in the world not to notice when he stopped going to soccer in the middle of the season.

Correction: I was the biggest moron in the world.

And to think, I had been furious at him when he hadn't noticed my braces.

"Matthew, I—"

"I don't want to hear it. But tell your friends. First of all, you need them, and second of all, they have to have noticed *something*. It's not like you're exactly subtle about your emotions, Claire."

"What are you talking about? I—"

He held up one hand, palm facing me. "Don't even."

I turned and started to walk away. Then Matthew said, "There's another thing, Claire. You have to spend some time with Dad."

"I—"

"Whatever you're going to say, I don't want to hear it. He has to be missing you. You know you've always been his favorite, right?"

"Me? You're the perfect one. You get the perfect grades, you have the perfect behavior, you're the one who's always the leader of every activity in the world, you win every trophy—how could *I* possibly be Dad's favorite? *You're* the one whose name he remembered, not me!"

Matthew chuckled. Like, in my face. Then he said, "Don't you get it? He calls me Matthew and you Piggy, right? That's because he never *made up* a nickname for me. I'm not trying to be a tool about this or anything, but—God! You don't even know what you have."

"Had."

"*Have.* He's not dead. He's right there."

"Yeah, but—you don't understand."

"Really? That's what you're going with?"

"Well, it's true. You don't."

"What don't I understand? I understand what it's like to have a dad who's had a stroke. I understand what it's like for my whole life to fall apart in a day. I understand what it means to give up everything I want to do for myself, just to be there for my parents. So where's the part I'm missing?"

"You don't—never mind."

"What?"

"Forget it."

"I can't just forget it. You said it. Now tell me."

"You don't know what it was *like*, Matthew. Being here. Watching it happen. Seeing the look on his face when *he* first realized what was happening. And I was so *scared*. Plus . . ."

"Plus what?"

"Plus, it was my fault!"

"What are you talking about, Claire?"

"The night before, I was having a stupid fight with Dad. And I said...I said, 'Maybe you need to struggle some more!'"

Matthew sighed. "Wow."

"Wow, what?" I asked.

"That's pretty bad. No wonder you've been staying away from Dad."

"I haven't been staying away from Dad!"

Matthew looked at me and raised one eyebrow, because, well, of *course* I had been staying away from our father.

"But," Matthew said, "just because you feel guilty doesn't mean you did this. I actually thought it was my fault for a while."

"Your fault? Why?"

"I said something mean to Dad over breakfast that morning, while you were asleep."

"You did?"

"Yeah. He asked if I wanted to see the new Iron Man movie together, and I said it looked stupid. I told Mom about the whole thing while Dad was in the hospital, and she said she was sure she and Dad had been obnoxious to their parents when they were teenagers, too. Then she told me that if obnoxious comments killed parents, every teenager in America would be an orphan."

"But I still feel so bad. I just can't believe that was the last thing I said to him."

"It wasn't. You've said tons of things to him since then. And you held his hand while he was having the stroke. I don't know if I could have done that."

"But still . . ."

"You know what, Claire? You can either mope forever or you can get past this and help out. Listen, I have a math test tomorrow that I haven't even started studying for yet. Why don't you go sit next to Dad, put your hand on his arm, and tell him about your day? Even if he doesn't understand every word, he definitely gets happier when you're in the room. And *I* get happier when I don't fail math tests."

I nodded, and Matthew took his school stuff up to his room.

I walked downstairs and sat down next to my father for the first time in weeks. He looked old to me—old and skinny. He was watching some kind of game show with flashing lights and a lot of shouting.

Before all this, I was pretty sure Dad had never watched a game show.

My heart was skipping and hammering in my chest, and I could feel my palms starting to sweat. This was insane! I was actually scared to sit next to my own father. I did the old three-inhalation trick from play rehearsals. Next, I ran both hands through my hair and tightened the hair tie that was holding it back away from my face. Finally, I took the remote control out of his hand, which was easy because his fingers were limp, and muted the sound on the TV.

"Hey, Daddy," I said, "the weirdest things have been going on in my life lately. Have you ever heard of Juan Cabrillo?"

15. Rock 'n' Drool

Just as I was starting to get used to the indignity of being fifth chair in band, which involved looking past another eighth grader and two seventh graders every time Ryder spoke to me in rehearsals, Mrs. Jones announced that we would be having auditions for jazz band right after Christmas vacation. This was bad, bad news, because there were only four altos in the jazz band.

Or, as Ryder so sweetly put it, "Do you know where the fifth-chair alto sits during jazz band performances? In your house!" Apparently, his post-stroke "Leave Claire Alone Period" was over.

I didn't know what to do. Now that I was trying to spend at least an hour or two a day with Dad so that Matthew could do more of his schoolwork, I didn't have time to practice. Plus, who was I kidding? I hadn't practiced since before the stroke anyway.

One day in the middle of science, Ryder started teasing me about how I wasn't going to make jazz band. I was actually in a group with him and Regina, which was entirely my fault. Mrs. Selinsky liked to change up the groups extremely often, and I had asked not to be put in a group with Jennifer or Desi because I was still mad at them from the braces incident. Jennifer had done this too many times before—she was very good at saying something mean, getting other girls to join in, and then afterward saying she hadn't meant anything by it.

Anyway, Roshni had stayed with Jennifer and Desi, so I was basically just a random, unwanted leftover when Mrs. Selinsky made up the new groups. Regina and Ryder were always stuck together like glue, and my super-excellent-luck powers planted me at a table with them. I was literally holding my breath as Mrs. Selinsky assigned the last few people, who were also all kind of random. It finally got down to just one kid: Christopher Marsh. I felt so sorry for him standing there. I mean, it wasn't his fault that he didn't understand how to talk to people. I had always tried to be nice to him in elementary school, but it was hard because he only knew how to discuss, like, three things.

The conversations would be like, "Hi, Christopher. How are you?"

"I am playing with glue. I enjoy playing with glue. I like to dry it partially and then roll it into balls."

"That's . . . nice. What did you pack for lunch? I have a yogurt."

"Yogurt is a bit like glue. Both are viscous, liquid suspensions."

"Um, okay."

"Also, glue is edible. I like it best when it is not quite dry."

What do you even say to that? I was like, "Want some gum?"

He said, "No, thank you. I have glue."

Anyway, Christopher was standing by the classroom door, just waiting to get assigned. I looked around, and every other group already had four kids in it. I thought, *Okay, Christopher's not so bad. He isn't mean to me, like Regina and Ryder, and he's great at anything that involves math. I can live with this.*

Then the classroom door opened, and Leigh barged in. Mrs. Selinsky snipped, "Nice of you to join us," and Leigh snarled back, "I know, right? Maybe if you're lucky, I'll give you some fashion tips while I'm here."

Roughly thirteen seconds later, I was perhaps the unhappiest member of an extremely mismatched group of five. We were supposed to do a pretty simple lab. All we had to accomplish by the end of class was to weigh a bunch of rocks, drop them one by one into a graduated cylinder full of water, and then calculate the density of each rock.

But of course, the work wasn't the hard part. Not killing each other was the challenge. Ryder immediately started in on me. He was all, "What's your audition piece gonna be—'Three Blind Mice'? 'Chopsticks'? The C scale?" I tried, as I always did, to ignore him and work on setting up a chart for our results with Regina, who was trying to get to work.

Leigh was in an unusually foul mood, even for her, and she started taking it out on Christopher. "Hey, Chris, I like your sweatpants. Did they come stained like that, or did you add the stains yourself?"

It was like watching someone smack a puppy. Christopher just sat there, kind of smiling. He totally didn't know what to do. Neither did I. First of all, I couldn't disengage from Ryder, and second of all, Leigh scared me. Not physically, but socially.

"And the way you pull them way up to your chest like that. I think that look might really catch on."

"Leave him alone, Leigh," Regina said.

I thought, *I was just about to say something.* I didn't really fool myself, though. I mostly just felt a flood of relief. My shirt was stuck to my back with sweat.

"I'm not bothering him. I'm complimenting him. You don't mind, do you, Chris?"

"My name is not Chris. It is Christopher."

"Oh, sweetie. I was just giving you a nickname because you're my friend. Don't you want to be my friend?" She was talking in a sort of flirty voice. She even leaned in to touch him.

Big mistake.

"Don't touch me. I don't like touching. No touching!" Christopher closed his eyes and began to rock forward and back. Regina stepped between Leigh and Christopher and hissed in Leigh's face, "Get on the other side of the table, you dumb little—"

And then Mrs. Selinsky was there. "Miss Chavez, what are you doing? Are you a troublemaker like your brother?"

"I don't know," Regina shot back. "Are you a trouble-maker like your *daughter?*"

We didn't manage to figure out the density of our rocks. It was basically a miracle that nobody started throwing them around the room.

. . . .

I really didn't want to get cut from jazz band, so I went to Mrs. Jones and asked her what I should do to practice for the auditions. She told me that the best thing I could do was work on sight-reading, tone, and fluency. I asked how to do that, and she handed me a huge book called *The Big Book of Pop Songs for Alto Sax.*

You had to kind of admire the creative title job, there.

Mrs. Jones told me that if I just learned to play as many different songs as possible, I would be preparing myself for the audition.

"This will get some tunes under your fingers. The more tunes you know, the better you'll play. Besides, you're depressed, Claire. Remember? You need to connect with the joy of making music again!"

I took the book, but inside I was still screaming, *I'm not depressed!*

. . . .

A few nights later, Mom had to run to the store, and Matthew was studying, so I was alone with Dad. I had already talked to him about everything I could think of, and he had responded by blurting various random nonsense words. It was still early, and I was bored, so I took out my sax and the new songbook and started playing.

Dad sat up straighter than he had in weeks, and looked right at me. You know how your parents sometimes tell you they're listening, but they're not actually listening? Maybe they're checking email, or texting, or paying bills, or writing something on a Post-it for your other parent, even as they insist you have their total, undivided attention?

Well, having a stroke does not generally improve the parental ability to focus. But apparently, certain music does.

My father had always loved 1960s music, and the first hundred or so songs in the book were all from that time. After a few songs, I could have sworn I heard him humming along, but then I thought it was probably my imagination. I stopped playing to see whether I was crazy.

As soon as I took the horn away from my lips, Dad pointed frantically at the book and grunted something that sounded like "Mo-ah mook!" I quickly started playing again, and by the end of that tune, I realized what he had been trying to say: "More music!"

The sixth song in the book was "Octopus's Garden" by the Beatles. Dad had always sung that one to me when I was little, and I could vividly remember wondering how a garden could grow under the sea. My lips were getting extremely fatigued, but I decided to try to get through it for him.

Dad started humming right away. By the second verse, he was tapping his good foot. By the third, he was banging his left hand against the arm of the sofa. A flicker of shadow on the wall behind him caught my eye, and I looked up from the page for a moment and saw that Matthew was standing at the top of the steps, smiling.

When I got to the end, Dad started singing the last line, over and over.

I took my mouthpiece away from my lips and sat there, stunned. Dad smiled and clapped. The clapping didn't work quite right, because his right hand was too floppy, but the intent was clear.

Matthew cleared his throat and said, "See? Toldja he missed you. Nice job, Piggy."

16. Good News, Bad News

Mom was pretty excited about Dad's musical break-through—so excited that she called the neurologist right away for an appointment. She thought this was going to be a major miracle and that Dad was about to start talking in complete, perfect sentences any minute.

The people at the neurology office were so, um, excited that they scheduled the appointment for only three weeks away. Evidently, this news wasn't so earth-shatteringly awesome to them.

In the meantime, I kept playing for my father, and found that there were several Beatles songs that made him sing along every time. He hadn't progressed to actually conversing about octopuses, gardens, twisting and shouting, or what was going to happen when he turned sixty-four, but Mom insisted it was just about to happen. I wasn't so sure, but at least it seemed to have given her some hope.

Then one day, she was in such a good mood that she answered the house phone when it rang, which she hadn't done for weeks. This was unfortunate timing, because the call was from Alanna's mom, who wanted to know whether we were all coming for Halloween. I was standing right there, which was the worst part. Mom's end of the discussion went like this:

"Hello, Susan. Yes, I know the Halloween party is coming up. I had just assumed you knew we weren't coming."

"Well, you know . . . we still aren't really getting out at this point."

"After David's *stroke*."

"In September. Oh my God. I just thought . . . I thought Claire must have told all her friends." As she said this, Mom gave me a look like, *We will discuss this later.*

"No, don't be sorry. It's not your fault. No, we don't need anything. We're managing. It hasn't been *easy*, but my parents and David's mother have been helping out a lot, and we have home health workers that stop by during the day. And the kids have been great."

"He can walk. And he can basically feed himself. But he can't speak, really. I know. Can you imagine David not being able to speak? David, of all people? It's like a punishment specifically designed for him. I'm sorry. I don't mean to . . ."

"Well, thank you."

"Thank you."

"Thank you."

"I don't *think* so, and she says she's not, but if you could just watch for any signs of that, I'd appreciate it."

"Thanks, we will."

"Five o'clock. Got it."

Then my mother hung up the phone, put her head in her hands, and cried.

So much for the whole "good mood" thing.

. . . .

The next time I had dance, my first session was a private with Miss Laura. I was super nervous about seeing my friends, who shared a break time with me right after the session. As I stretched, I tried extremely hard to clear my mind. One of the other teachers, Miss Amy, always said, "If your thoughts are light, your feet will be light."

But Miss Laura was *not* Miss Amy. She was working with me on a few different combinations for my classes. On this night, I couldn't even get through one combination without her stopping me to lay on a barrage of criticism. She kept saying things like "*Finish* your turns, Claire! I wish you could see how great Alanna is at this now. She *always* finishes her turns. Maybe she can show you after class." Then, when I went back to try again, I would concentrate on my turns, but she would go, "Extension! I want to see extension. Your arms, your legs—everything should be at *full* extension! You should ask your friend Katherine for help with this. She has the most lovely extension."

In case it wasn't awful enough having to be in the baby classes while my friends were in the high school group, getting my nose rubbed in all the reasons *why* I was inferior was kind of the cherry on the crap cake.

During break, I just wanted to avoid everybody, sit in the corner, and eat my miserable dinner of yogurt and a thermos of instant soup. But of course Alanna and Katherine had to come rushing over and throw their arms around me. It was only my incredibly quick reflexes that saved us all from getting ultrahot, noodly broth all over our dance outfits.

Which might have been less painful than having to go through the whole "Oh my gosh I'm so sorry about your dad why didn't you tell us" sobfest that followed. Right in the middle of the lobby. While all the high school girls watched disdainfully from one end, the babies from my classes stared in horror from the other, and a gaggle of assorted dance moms kept sneaking glances and whispering in the middle. We might as well have just set up a *Watch the Crying Girls: Only Five Cents!* booth at a carnival. At least then we might have earned some nickels.

By the time I got called in for my next class, I felt like I had been spray-painted with a sticky mixture of hair product, tears, makeup, and, quite possibly, snot.

I didn't feel beautiful, and I certainly didn't feel like a great dancer, but in a strange way, I did kind of feel loved.

. . . .

Our Halloween sleepover started out absolutely swell. When my mom dropped me off, there was the awkward part when Katherine's and Alanna's moms both hugged me, told me I could come to them if I needed anything—*anything*—and then shared some kind of deeply significant "Watch out for Claire" eye-contact moment.

Did these people think I was blind?

Then there was the costume situation. Alanna was decked out in a Marilyn Monroe outfit, complete with white dress, pearls, and a fake fur coat. Katherine was a black cat, which meant a bodysuit, black leg warmers, a black hat with ears attached, and a black scarf. I was the only moron who didn't think about the fact that it would be twenty-three degrees and sleeting while we trick-or-treated, so I was sporting my tap-dance costume from last year's recital, which was made of thin material, had short sleeves, and stopped above my knees. I was supposed to be Rosie the Riveter, but instead I felt like Patty the Popsicle.

Still, I was determined to have fun, so I set out with a smile plastered on my face and kept it there even as my teeth chattered so hard I thought my braces might come flying off from the vibration. By the time we got back to the house and made it upstairs to Alanna's room, I could barely force my fingers to unclench from around my candy bag so that we could pour everything out and see what we'd gotten. We had a tradition of lighting a bunch of candles, and then comparing our loot in the dim light.

That was when the others noticed how cold I was. They wrapped me up in a blanket, and after a while, some feeling came back to my extremities, which was nice. The oddest sensation was in my mouth, which had gotten so cold that I could actually feel the pain from the icy metal of my braces touching me.

That didn't go away until Alanna's mom came up with cups of warm cider. I swished my first sip around my mouth until my wires were all heated up. I know—weird, right?

Then I took stock of my candy situation, and wanted to throw a crying fit like a little kid. I couldn't eat a single freaking thing on that floor. Everything had caramel, peanuts, crunchy this, extra-gooey that—an orthodontic nightmare. The candy was so useless to me for eating purposes, I might as well have just gone door to door asking Alanna's neighbors for razor blades and bottles of expired medication.

I was tempted to go back out and ask for those once Alanna and Katherine started chowing down on the candy I couldn't eat, while gossiping about the girls I didn't know in the class I wasn't allowed to attend. It was like I wasn't even in the room.

Katherine said, "Alanna, could you believe it when Janna texted Jeff a dinner order in the middle of class?"

I said, "Uh, who's Jeff?"

Alanna said, "Her boyfriend. I KNOW! And then HE ACTUALLY CAME WITH THE FOOD! She's always doing stuff like that. It's exactly like Madison always says."

And then they both chanted at the exact same time, in the exact same singsongy voice: "If Janna texted Jeff to stop breathing right now, he'd text back three minutes later and ask for permission to die."

I just kind of sat there, like, *Wow, this would be so super funny if I . . . umm . . . knew or cared about any of these people.* The torment went on and on, until suddenly Katherine noticed that I hadn't said anything in a while.

And that I was tearing the wrapper of the one candy I could eat (a plain chocolate bar) into smaller and smaller pieces.

And that I was chewing on my hair, which I only do when I am really upset.

And, okay, there might have been some small amount of leakage emitting from the inside corners of my eye areas.

"Claire?" she whispered. "Are you all right?"

I wanted to scream, *Am I all right? Do I look all right? Would you be all right if you couldn't dance, you couldn't play your instrument, everyone at your school hated you, your friends pitied you, and your father lost his ability to do—oh, I don't know—basically everything?*

But I thought that might sound too dramatic, so I just cleared my throat and said, "I'm fine. It's just, uh, the candle smell. I must be allergic. Are these candles floral scented or something?"

Because, you know, a lot of times the symptoms of allergic reaction include teary eyes and blatant psychosis.

Alanna and Katherine gave each other the same look their moms had exchanged earlier, and then Katherine said she had to go to the bathroom. *Ah, I get it,* I thought. *She's going to go tell the mothers I'm depressed. But I am not depressed—I'm mad! Why can't anybody tell the difference around here?*

. . . .

I went with my parents to my father's neurologist appointment. Mom insisted I had to come and bring my sax, in case the doctor needed to see Dad's singing. I was like, *Yeah, I'm sure you can't just* say *he's been belting out "Yellow Submarine" every night. The quality of his Ringo Starr impression might be of extreme diagnostic importance.* With a cane and some help from Mom, Dad was able to walk out to the car, which was great. I was shocked to realize that I hadn't actually been in a car with him since the ride home from the hospital.

I couldn't stand being trapped in the house for a long weekend. I wondered what a couple of months, mostly in one room, would feel like. Mom had been trying for a while to get Dad out of the house, but he kept refusing to go anywhere. It was terrible. The whole thing made me want to reach out, hold my father's hand, and never let go.

Once, when I was in kindergarten, I had the flu and missed a few days of school. I remembered two things about it quite vividly. The first was throwing up while my father held my hair away from my face. His hand had been cool against my cheek, and then, when he handed me a cup of water to wash my mouth out, he had brushed the backs of his fingers against my forehead.

The second was that I slept a lot, but whenever I was awake, my dad was there to entertain me. We played with my ponies, cuddled up and watched movies, read together, and drew pictures. We even made a blanket fort that took up the entire living room. When my mom got home from work at the end of the third day, she asked how things were going, and I said, "Excellent! I think Daddy should be my teacher from now on!"

Mom and Dad had looked at each other all mushily, and I had covered my eyes in case they were going to kiss.

The point is, the memory made me realize how much more I owed my father. I vowed that, as long as he was semi-helpless, I was going to make his life better.

We were in the waiting room for forty-five minutes, which is an extremely long time to sit with a person who can't hold a normal conversation, although my dad seemed to be pretty delighted by the madcap excitement of the twenty-four-hour news channel, which was blaring from a TV in one corner. From what I could tell, something had blown up in the Middle East, there was extreme weather somewhere else, something big had happened in the stock market, lots of earthquake refugees looked extremely miserable in a muddy place, and the president's office was going to make a major announcement about something-something soon.

It was hard to get the details, because Dad kept poking my arm and saying, "Portant! Portant!" Mom felt that this was yet another sign of massive communication-related progress.

The doctor was less impressed, although at least he didn't make me run out to the car for my saxophone. He said it was an "established phenomenon" for people with left-hemisphere strokes to be able to sing songs they had known well before, even when they couldn't speak with much coherency otherwise.

Mom asked, "But isn't this a sign of progress?"

The doctor said, "Maybe."

She said, "And he's starting to get close to saying other words in context. Isn't that right, Claire?"

I said, "Uh, I think so. Wait, what does that mean, exactly?"

"You know, like when he poked you and said, 'Portant,' in the waiting room. He was definitely trying to tell you the news was important. Right?"

"I think so, Mom."

My mother turned to the doctor and said, "So you see, he's definitely improving, but I admit the progress is . . . well, it's slower than we'd like. Are there some additional things we can do to help this process along?"

The neurologist took off his glasses with one hand, and rubbed the bridge of his nose with the other. *Crud*, I thought. *There's no way that's a positive sign.*

Next, he called the nurse back in. "Mr. Goldsmith," he said, "would you please take a little walk down the hall with my nurse, Alison? She's just going to see how well you are getting around."

Mom touched Dad's knee and said, "It's okay, honey. You can go with her."

The doctor waited until the door closed behind Dad before he spoke. "Mrs. Goldsmith, more than this cognitive piece, I am extremely concerned about your husband's weight. He's lost twenty-seven pounds in two months. If you can't reverse this trend immediately, I'm afraid you aren't going to be able to maintain your husband at home."

"What are you talking about?"

"I'm talking about a nursing home placement. That might be temporary or it might be permanent. But right now, your husband is literally wasting away. Now, I'm going to prescribe a medication to increase his appetite, and I am also going to write down the name of a nutritional shake I want your husband to drink every day between lunch and dinner. When you go to check out, they will call over to your husband's primary care doctor and schedule a follow-up appointment for three days from now. This is the kind of decision we will all have to make together as a team, but you and your husband are the ones who have the most direct control over the results. You have to do whatever it takes to increase his food intake."

Mom and the doctor kept talking about the details, but I kind of zoned out at that point, because my father came back in. I looked at his cheekbones and his neck and his elbows. I noticed how his clothing was hanging off him loosely. I didn't think it had always done that. He noticed me looking and smiled at me, the same smile he had always turned my way whenever I needed him.

That was the moment I stopped being angry.

And started being depressed.

17. The Year We Stuffed Dad for Thanksgiving

So the mission at home changed completely overnight, from entertaining Dad and trying to get him to talk, to Operation: Weight Gain. Every meal went from excruciatingly long to ultra-excruciatingly long. Then there were the between-meal shakes, the snacks, and Mom's "spontaneous" nightly ice-cream parties. There were also supposed to be major changes to Dad's exercise plans in order to build up his muscles and increase his appetite, but when I asked one night how that was all going, Mom just said, "Eat your ice cream before it melts, Claire Bear."

Things got so desperate on the food front that one evening, when we were all in the car on our way home from one of Dad's appointments, Mom suddenly swerved into the parking lot of a donut shop and said, "Guess what, kids? It's snack time!"

Matthew, who's the King of Schedules, said, "No, it's not. It's dinnertime."

Mom reached into the backseat, grabbed his leg, and nodded in Dad's direction. Matthew got the hint and said, "I mean, yay! Snack time for everyone!"

Dad looked kind of panicky at the thought of going into the shop. It had been months since all of us had been out in a public place together, plus he had to know how obvious his eating struggles were to anybody who was watching. Still, the donut place seemed like a pretty perfect choice. You didn't even need utensils to eat a donut. All you had to do was grab and bite.

Mom smiled a huge, fake smile, hurried around the car to Dad's side, and said, "Let's go, honey! This will be fun!"

Mom practically skipped into the store, if it's possible to skip while dragging a shuffling man. Matthew and I kind of slunk in behind them. I was praying we wouldn't see anybody we knew.

Mom got us a table and positioned Matthew, Dad, and me in seats. Then she went to the counter and ordered donuts and drinks. When he first caught sight of the food on the table, Dad looked pretty excited. But then he tried to grab a Boston cream donut, and his thumb squished its way right through the dough part and into the filling. This made him try to drop the donut, but it was sort of impaled on his finger. He started shaking his hand, and didn't stop until the entire pastry flew off and landed on the floor several feet away.

Needless to say, the situation didn't improve. The final score of our outing was Floor 3, Dad's Mouth 0. We were finally forced to flee in despair.

On the way out, I noticed the strangest thing. My father almost seemed to be smiling, just the slightest little bit, as though he had intentionally sabotaged the whole adventure.

When we weren't out on disastrous fried-dough missions, I still kept playing the sax for my father whenever I could, and Matthew borrowed a book of Beatles songs for trumpet, so our house sounded a lot more cheerful than it actually was.

In my downtime, all I wanted to do was lie on my bed and stare at the wall. I stopped returning texts from friends and dropped out of sight on social media. It was like, *What's the point?* Everybody else would be posting pictures of their healthy, happy families going away for the weekend, or making witty comments about their fathers' Halloween costumes, and what was I going to do—put up a selfie of me and my dad in matching drool bibs?

Leigh Monahan would have loved that.

At school, and even at dance, everything was just a big ball of blah. Mostly, I spent my time fighting an overwhelming urge to curl up in a ball and do nothing. Everything looked gray. All my favorite foods tasted gray. My friends were annoying without meaning to be, and my enemies—ugh. Teachers who didn't notice my mood were awful, but teachers who did notice and tried to be extra kind to me were even worse. I almost appreciated the steady, routine terribleness of Mrs. Selinsky, because at least I knew I'd never have to pretend to be thankful to her or say, "Oh, it's nothing, I'm fine."

Because I wasn't fine. My father was starving to death, apparently, and if we didn't keep jamming food down his throat every second, he was going to have to go live in some kind of nursing home.

Making him eat was so sad. He clearly didn't *want* to. He was so tired, and chewing took so much effort. The shakes were easier for him to swallow, but I tried a bit of one and it tasted like very slightly flavored chalk. We would all sit around the table, pretending to be excited about every morsel, as if he was some two-year-old. I kept waiting for my mom to go, "Here comes the airplane, open up the hangar!"

When Dad had *really* had it, sometimes he would literally cover his mouth and whimper.

It hurt to see my father like that. Some part of me wanted him to jump up out of his seat, roar with rage, and

165

knock all the food off the table. At least then, he would be fighting instead of acting so helpless.

In the middle of all this, Mom had insisted on hosting Thanksgiving. I thought she was nuts, and even Matthew argued against it, but all she said was, "Your father deserves a nice holiday meal with his family, and this will be easier on him than trying to travel." She had a point, but still . . . I was expecting the worst Thanksgiving of my life. I mean, I hate turkey with a burning passion that defies all explanation every year, but I usually love the sweet potatoes with marshmallows, the stuffing, the mashed potatoes, and my all-time favorite: the green-bean casserole. Plus, there are all the desserts we have only once a year, like pumpkin pie and pumpkin roll. I usually love seeing my whole extended family, hearing what everyone is thankful for, and playing with all the little cousins all day.

But I found myself dreading the event because, for one thing, while my dad's mother and sister had obviously both seen him since the stroke, none of my cousins had. They lived a couple of hours away, and we hadn't exactly been inviting people over right and left. I had a feeling some of them were going to freak out and make a scene. And then there was the stupid going-around-the-table-and-being-thankful scene. What was I supposed to say? "I'm thankful that Dad's stroke wasn't the fatal bleeding kind"?

There were days when I wasn't even sure this was better for him. He couldn't do his work, he couldn't do anything for his family, he couldn't even get a meatball from his plate to his mouth. If I were being a hundred percent honest, I couldn't really say I was thankful he was alive in this condition.

Besides, what was the next kid going to follow that with? "I'm thankful for rainbows and unicorns! Please pass the squash-and-apple casserole"?

The whole thing was just the setup for a nightmare, and that was before Mom put Dad's entire dinner in the blender. What came pouring out was the most revolting glop I'd ever witnessed. You know the reindeer poop they sell at Christmastime? Well, this stuff was the Thanksgiving equivalent—turkey vomit. It featured little foamy bits of marshmallow on top, and smelled vaguely of both overcooked bird and cinnamon.

You should have seen Dad's face when everybody else got an overflowing plate of sliced poultry with all the trimmings, and he got a steaming mug of the liquefied version. His eyes got all squinched up, his cheeks flushed red, his teeth clenched, and his nose wrinkled up. He even clenched both fists, although the right one was admittedly not super tight. Anyway, this was the one time since September that he had been able to express his feelings perfectly without words.

167

Mom didn't make us go around and say anything. Instead, she just said, very quietly, "I'm thankful for all of you—your love, your support—and David and I are so glad that we can all gather together around a warm table, especially at this difficult time. Now, come on— eat." I don't know who else noticed, but for a while after that, she kept wiping her eyes when she thought nobody was looking.

Dad had gotten pretty good at using his special fat-handled spoons, and rarely had problems eating if we were careful about what we gave him, and as long as he did everything slowly and carefully. I don't know if it was the distraction of all the people around the table, the emotion of the holiday, or the disgustingness of his actual food, but all of a sudden, halfway through the meal, he went into a massive coughing fit.

Matthew and Mom both patted him on the back, and Gram jumped up from her seat and scurried over to him, but he seemed to be okay after a couple of minutes, and people started talking around the table again. The main strategy was apparently to pretend this was a normal holiday dinner, so the little kids got loud and laughed too much, my aunts and uncles all pretended their misbehavior was super cute, our older cousins blabbed on and on about how miserable high school was and/or how amazing college was, and the adults discussed sensitive political topics.

The political talk was the worst, because normally my father would have been the fiery liberal in the mix, but this year, my most right-wing uncle was all, "More guns! Less government! Yay, white people!" and Dad couldn't challenge anything he said. I looked at Dad and tried to judge whether he understood the conversation. I noticed his eyes were squinty again, and the good side of his mouth was curled into a snarl.

He understood enough.

Well, at least that was a positive sign from a medical point of view, as long as he didn't have another stroke from the frustration of listening to the extreme opposite of every view he had, without being able to say anything back.

Then a semi-amazing thing happened. Matthew jumped in. He started hurling statistics, historical facts, and quotes from the Founding Fathers at my uncle. It was surprisingly similar to watching my father in action. Dad even reached over and patted Matthew's arm, which made everybody laugh.

Mom took that as her cue to break up the battle by serving dessert. But actually, I had been loving the display. Usually, I was the bigmouthed one. It was kind of sweet to see Matthew take the heat while I sat back with imaginary popcorn and watched. My first thought was *Hey, Dad would have been proud.* My second thought was *No. Dad is proud.*

. . . .

The day after Thanksgiving seemed pretty normal, or at least it was our new normal, but on Saturday morning, Dad woke up coughing. At first, we thought it was just a cold. But by Sunday night, he had a fever. On Monday morning, Mom told us she was taking him to the emergency room.

I asked whether I could stay home from school to go with them, but she told me I should just go to school, because "there's no use worrying" and "it might be nothing." Meanwhile, my father was shivering uncontrollably, doubling over with coughing fits, and sweating like he had just run a marathon.

Matthew just shrugged, said, "Okay," and marched off to school. He's always been the good listener in the family.

I'm not Matthew, though. So yeah, I *definitely* wasn't going to be worrying while I was in school. And I was *sure* my dad hacking up a lung probably wasn't going to turn out to be anything serious. I started arguing. But Mom finally just said, "We don't have time for this. Listen, bring your phone to school and leave it on vibrate. I promise I'll text you updates when I can, and I'll send one of your grandparents to get you if anything urgent is going on. Okay?"

"But I'm not allowed to use my phone in class. I'll get in trouble." This was true. The teachers on my team went berserk if they saw a kid with a phone. Whipping out your phone in class was like holding up a KICK ME! sign at a karate tournament.

"If you get in trouble, I'll stick up for you. Now help me get your father into the car."

So I did. As I attached his seat belt, I whispered, "I love you, Daddy," and kissed his forehead. It was hot and damp and tasted like salt. He moaned and his eyes rolled.

Don't worry, my butt, I thought.

I checked my phone every thirty seconds all day, but of course nothing happened until the worst possible time—science class. I kept thinking I felt the vibrations, and pulling the phone out under my desk, or asking to go to the bathroom and then checking, but there was nothing. Then I would torture myself, like, *If she hasn't texted, is that a good thing or a bad thing? Maybe he's fine, but as long as she took the day off from work, she's getting him a haircut and some new clothes, so she just forgot to call. They're probably just out getting some nice, soft ice cream—Dad loves soft ice cream.*

No, who am I kidding? He was wearing filthy sweats. Even if he somehow got cured on the way to the hospital, Mom would never take him out in public in sweats. Besides, lack of texts is definitely a bad sign. Mom likes giving good news, and hates messing with our school days. She's probably sitting there right now next to Dad's lifeless body, going, "Well, sure, he's dead, and the kids technically have a right to know. But they can't do anything about it right now, and I'd hate to disrupt the educational process."

So there I was, watching Mrs. Selinsky hop up and down on one foot and gesture wildly like some crazed witch doctor—which I was somewhat sure was her attempt to teach us something about the concept of gravity, somehow—and resisting the urge to slip my phone ever so slightly out of my pants pocket. That's when all h-e-double-hockey-sticks broke loose. The PA system crackled to life, and the principal's booming voice, which was pretty pumped-up on a normal day, practically shattered the speakers:

ATTENTION ALL STUDENTS AND STAFF. THIS IS A LOCKDOWN. I REPEAT, THIS IS A LOCKDOWN. THIS IS NOT A DRILL. YOU WILL ALL SHELTER IN PLACE UNTIL YOU ARE GIVEN FURTHER INSTRUCTIONS BY AN ADMINISTRATOR OR EMERGENCY SERVICES PERSONNEL.

I had been vaguely aware that something was missing from my day, and after the announcement, I knew what that something had been: raw terror. I looked around, and almost every student in the room appeared to be as panicked as I felt. Ryder's head was twitching back and forth. He looked like a rabbit trying to watch a Ping-Pong match. Roshni was staring at me, mouthing, *What's happening?* I shrugged. Jennifer and Desi were hugging each other.

Barf.

The only two calm people were Regina and Leigh. Regina just sat there, cracking a big old piece of against-the-rules bubble gum. Leigh was flipping through a fashion magazine under her desk and didn't even seem to have noticed that class had been interrupted.

Meanwhile, Mrs. Selinsky was scrambling around the room, flipping off all the lights (which made Leigh mutter,

"Hey!"), pulling down all the window shades, and locking the only door. Then she told us all to huddle together in the corner of the room against the hallway wall, farthest from the door.

I had just scrunched down next to Roshni when my phone buzzed. I took it out as subtly as I could. The message could have been better:

Sweetie, your father has pneumonia. The doctors think he must have inhaled some food when he had that coughing fit at Thanksgiving. He is being admitted to the intensive care unit. Grandpa just picked up Matthew and is on his way to get you right now. Then you will all come here.

That's when I heard the sirens. It sounded like every police car, fire truck, and ambulance in town must have been outside our school. I looked up and saw the swirling lights from lots of emergency vehicles sweeping the spaces between the windows and the shades. About a minute later, a *whup-whup* sound joined the general echoing chaos.

"Holy cow," Ryder said. "That's gotta be a police helicopter."

All I could think was, *That's what my mom gets for her stupid optimism.* She had been wrong about everything. My dad wasn't okay. Somebody was disrupting the crap out of my educational process. And I had a feeling my grandpa wasn't going to be taking me *anywhere.*

18. Not Very Meredith

Mrs. Selinsky's next step was to reorganize our squatting positions so that we were with our lab groups. Because moving us all around in the dark made a lot of sense. Also because, you know, in a potential bomb, mass shooting, or hostage situation, that was definitely going to increase our chances of survival. I could picture it. Mrs. Selinsky, heroic teacher, would be interviewed on the seven o'clock news, and the reporter would ask, "How did you stay so calm during the crisis?"

Mrs. S would say, "Well, I thought of my daughter, Meredith, and that put me in my happy place."

Then the reporter would say, "Remarkable. And what gave you the brilliant idea of placing the students in their lab groups?"

Mrs. S would grin her slightly demented grin, leap up on top of the news desk, and say, "Because you never know when you might have to analyze the mass of a bunch of different minerals using the water-displacement method, and if it came down to that, I wanted the kids in their most experienced configurations. Plus, I hate everyone at Claire Goldsmith's table and wanted to make them suffer."

The reporter would raise one eyebrow, inch her chair slowly away from Mrs. S, and say, "So there you have it, America. One brave teacher, an inspiring daughter, and a bunch of wet rocks."

My group ended up smushed against a super-hot radiator, in case the general stuffiness of the room, and the sweat of a class of panicking eighth graders, weren't uncomfortable enough. I also noticed that someone—or quite possibly several someones—wasn't a big fan of deodorant.

So, yay for lockdowns.

I held my phone way down behind Leigh's back and texted Matthew:

Tell G-pa to forget about picking me up. School on lockdown, don't know why. You go right to hosp. Hug Dad for me.

Because I am a hero.

Then I tried to cry quietly. Because I was overwhelmed and terrified.

I wasn't the only one crying or texting. A bunch of kids were laughing, or complaining about how they were going to be late for after-school stuff if this went on too long, but several kids had covered their faces with their hands, and I could also detect the telltale blue glow of phone screens coming up from laps.

It was pretty obvious with the lights off, even with the rotating light patterns on the walls from outside.

Kids were also whispering about the texts they were getting. Here are some of the things I heard within the first three minutes:

"There's a shooter in the building!"

"There are bombs in both gyms!"

"False alarm!"

"There's a terrorist attack going on downtown. City hall is under attack!" (Yeah, because the world's terrorists are keenly aware that the nerve center of America's might is the city hall of Bethlehem, PA.)

"Some lady is giving birth in the cafeteria!" (Which would cause a lockdown *how?*)

"The principal's toupee is on fire!" (Funny, but again— how would this result in a lockdown?)

Then Mrs. S announced, "Turn off your cell phones!"

Leigh said, "What? You can't make us turn off our phones! Our parents make us carry them for emergencies, and this is an emergency!"

"But you are using them *during class*, and that's against

the rules! Now, don't make me come over there, Leigh Monahan!"

Regina muttered, "I bet *Meredith* never used her phone during class."

"WHAT did you say, Miss Chavez?"

"Nothing."

"Excellent. Now turn off your phones."

Like five different kids said, "But—"

"NOW!" Mrs. Selinsky screeched. I was sort of hoping she would attempt to jump up on a table, miss, and do a Cabrillo. Because there was no way I was turning my phone off.

Some of the other students must have obeyed, but at least one kid on the other side of the group didn't, because a few minutes later, Mrs. Selinsky yelled, "Is that a glowing rectangle in your pocket?"

"Or are you just happy to see me?" Ryder mumbled.

A bunch of us snickered, and then Mrs. S really lost it. She started screaming and yelling at the top of her lungs about disrespect and how she was sick of having her authority undermined, blah blah blah, Meredith, yada yada. The only good part of this insane tirade was that I figured she was distracted enough that I could sneak a peek at my phone again. Sure enough, there was a message from Matthew:

Nothing to worry about at your school. Just a bank robbery on Easton Ave. Crazy. Bad news here, tho. Dad got a breathing treatment and oxygen, and is still having trouble breathing after. They are sending him in for a scan now. Everybody rushing.

I tucked my phone into the pocket of my hoodie and looked up to find that Roshni was arguing with Mrs. S. I knew she had said she would eventually, but this was still extremely unusual—Roshni got the best grades in the class and never, ever got in trouble. She said her parents would kill her if she did. The day was turning out to be special for everybody.

"What did you say to me, young lady?"

"I said, should you really be yelling right now? Aren't we supposed to be quiet during a shelter-in-place drill?"

"*You* are. *I'm* the teacher."

"Okay. So if a maniac with a gun is running around and hears you screaming, he won't come in and kill us all because *you're the teacher*? That's the stupidest thing I've ever heard."

I was like, *Whoa, Roshni.* Mrs. Selinsky lifted her arm way up over her head, as though she was planning to fling a lightning bolt down at Roshni, but then she just dropped her arm and turned away. The whole class was silent for a while after that, because (A) I think that level of student-teacher confrontation is sort of scary, and (B) so is the idea of a school shooter. I wondered whether I should tell everyone what Matthew had written. But then I realized I couldn't, because then Mrs. S would take away my phone.

Mrs. S had moved as far from the class as she could, and my group was in the corner of the class farthest from her. Leigh's head was only a few inches in front of mine, and Ryder and Regina were between me and the corner of the room. Christopher was on the other side of me; I suddenly noticed that his arms were hugged tightly around himself. I realized this must be a nightmare for him, because he hated being too close to other people so much. I whispered to him, "Christopher, it's okay. I just found out that the school is safe. I bet we'll get let out soon."

"What is soon? A week? A day? An hour?"

"I bet we'll be out in less than an hour."

"How do you know?" Christopher said, too loudly. He had never really caught on to the whole concept of whispering. In elementary school, our teachers had constantly been telling him to use his inside voice.

"Shhh! Don't say anything after I tell you this, but my

brother texted me. He must have checked online. He doesn't go to this school."

"NO TEXTING! NO TEXTING IS A RULE!" Thankfully, a new bunch of sirens had started wailing just as he started to say this, or I'd have been doomed.

"Shhh! I know, but my dad is in the hospital."

"Your dad is an author. He writes books."

"That's true."

Ryder tapped me on the shoulder. "Why is your dad in the hospital, Claire?" he asked.

I bit my lip. On a normal day, Ryder wasn't exactly my first choice of confidant. On the other hand, this wasn't exactly a normal day. "He has pneumonia. It's really bad. Matthew says they're doing some kind of scan right now. I don't know what's happening. They were on their way to get me when the lockdown started, and now—"

My phone vibrated again in my pocket. I took it out. I had a new message from my brother:

I don't think the scan was good. I'm not sure, but I think they are taking Dad to surgery.

Regina leaned over Ryder and read the text. "Wow, Starbuck," she said, "this is serious. What can we do?"

I couldn't believe it. Regina was offering to help me. But unless she was secretly a lung surgeon with teleportation powers, I wasn't so sure how much she could actually do. I realized I was crying again.

Great.

Christopher started tapping on my shoulder repeatedly. I looked at him.

In the same semi-robotic tone he always had, he said, "I am patting you. My mother says that people pat their friends during times of great distress. And she says crying is a sign of great distress. Do not worry. I will protect you."

"Thanks, Christopher," I managed to choke out. Then Mrs. S appeared and demanded, "Phone. Now!"

"Shhh!" Roshni said from across the room.

While Mrs. S was looking over there, Ryder got up and stood between me and Mrs. Selinsky. "You don't understand," he said. "This is a real emergency. Please don't take Claire's phone. Her father is in the emergency room. He's about to go into surgery."

Even in the dim light, I could see the sneer on Mrs. S's face. "Rules are rules, and you were all warned," she said.

"Then take my phone. I don't care. But let her keep hers."

"Were you using your phone?"

"Well, no."

"Then I don't want *your* phone. I want Claire's phone."

"You can't do this. Listen. When Meredith was in school, if you were in the hospital, would you have wanted a teacher to take away her phone?"

"How DARE you bring up my daughter to me?" Mrs. Selinsky was in full-on scary mode again. I mean, she had only been, like, half a heartbeat away from lunatic status this whole time, but now it was *on*. "Don't you ever mention her name again. Now get out of my way and sit down!"

But Regina jumped up and stood next to Ryder. "He didn't do anything wrong. Now, why don't you just walk away? Where's your heart? All you have to do is let this girl keep her phone on so she knows what's happening to her dad."

Mrs. Selinsky stood there, glaring at Regina and Ryder. I noticed that Regina had put her hand on Ryder's shoulder, and that all three of them were breathing hard. Meanwhile, Christopher was still frantically patting me, almost hard and fast enough to distract me from the pounding of my heart.

Then my phone lit up again.

Mrs. Selinsky moved so fast, I wasn't even sure until afterward that I had seen her hand coming at me. She snatched my phone before I could even read the message on the screen. I reached for it, and she slapped my hand. The sound was like a shot in the enclosed space, which made me realize the sirens had all stopped.

Ryder began to grab at Mrs. Selinsky's hands, but Regina's voice was faster than his fingers.

"Hey, give her the phone back, you crazy BEEP!" Regina said. Well, she didn't exactly say BEEP, but the word *did* start with a *B*.

If the whole class hadn't already been staring at us in horror after the slap, they were definitely staring now. It felt to me like the whole world stopped for a moment, until finally Mrs. Selinsky said, "She will have to see the principal for it tomorrow. You will *all* be seeing the principal tomorrow. I would imagine some suspensions will be in order."

About five minutes later, we got the all-clear signal. Nobody said a word on the way out of the room, but several kids ran up to me in the hall to offer their phones. By then I felt like I would explode if I didn't leave the building, so I just ran home without even stopping at my locker, and called Matthew from there.

Grandma came to get me. My grandparents' house is only about seven minutes from ours, but those seven minutes felt longer than the entire lockdown had. And the thirteen-minute trip to the hospital was even worse. I kept wanting to scream, *This car has a gas pedal—use it!*

Because if your dad were in the intensive care unit, hooked up to oxygen machines and feeding tubes, and you had been kept away from him all day, you'd be in a hurry, too. It's funny—before this year, getting suspended would have been, like, my greatest fear in the world. But the fear of getting suspended tomorrow means nothing if your father might be dying today.

19. What Comes After Mayhem Monday

The longer you sit there watching someone you love struggling to breathe, the worse it gets. The suspense just builds and builds. By the way, when you hear that cliché— "struggle to breathe"—you probably don't really appreciate what it means unless you've watched someone do it. The sounds are awful. You've got the nonstop, low-level hiss of the oxygen, the cracking and wheezing as the person inhales and exhales, and the booming, wet, splatty sounds when he bursts into coughing fits every few minutes. Those fits are generally followed by loud beeping as the machines all go haywire because of the coughing, which brings the nurses running in to check and then reset everything.

So everybody settles back in until the next spasm of choking hacks.

Oh, and there are the visuals. Aside from the blinking machines and dripping tubes, there was the awful gray color of my father's skin, the exhausting contortions his shoulders and ribs went through every time he inhaled, the blue of his lips, and the sweat running down his shrunken-looking face.

He almost didn't even look like my dad. He looked like a voodoo-doll puppet of my dad that some horrible evil magician was torturing. But then, once in a while, when he opened his eyes and groaned, the tone of his voice and the little bit of that panicked look we had all learned to recognize forced me to admit that—yes—this was really happening to my real-life dad.

It wasn't voodoo, it was just the delayed end result of Dad's Thanksgiving smoothie.

Mom didn't look or sound much better than Dad at this point, but she still kept sending me to school every morning. Somehow, Matthew and I got booted out of the room when visiting hours ended, but she never seemed to leave Dad's side. Grandma and Grandpa might as well have installed a taxi meter in their car and a hotel reception desk in their front hall, because they became our transport and room-and-board system again.

I figured it was best not to mention the whole Selinsky debacle when I finally got to the hospital after the lockdown. Mom seemed relieved I hadn't been shot, held hostage, or blown up, so I just left things right there for a while. She did say something about how I should call her from my cell if I needed anything, and I sort of nodded and smiled on my way out with my grandpa.

It seemed rather unlikely that Mrs. S was going to use my phone to call Mom, because my phone was password protected, but I was pretty sure this would all catch up with me in the morning. Still, when I closed my eyes to go to sleep, I didn't think about her or school. I heard my father's raspy, strained breathing in my head, and prayed and prayed that he would have the strength to keep on going.

. . . .

I was not hugely surprised when my entire science group got called out of first period to the principal's office. Roshni grabbed my hand and squeezed it as I walked past her desk on the way out, but strangely, I didn't really feel like I needed to be comforted. I didn't much care about what happened to me, although I did want my phone back. Maybe I was too tired, or maybe I had been through too much, but this almost felt as if it was happening to somebody else.

It was definitely happening to Christopher, who looked miserable. He kept pulling up his pants—although if they went any higher, he was going to hang himself with his belt—and muttering under his breath. I said to him,

"Christopher, what are you saying? Are you worried? Everything is going to be all right. You didn't do anything wrong yesterday."

"I know," he said. "But you are going to get in trouble. My mother told me that protecting friends is a rule, and I did not protect you."

"You tried, though. Listen, it's impossible to protect people sometimes, but you were there for me."

Leigh snickered. "Oh, that's sooo dramatic! You were *there for me*. Someone get me a bucket. I'm going to throw up."

Ryder stepped out in front of all of us, turned, and blocked Leigh's path. "What's wrong with you, Leigh?" he asked. "Just because nobody actually cares about you, that doesn't mean we're all as lonely and bitter as you are."

"For *real*," Regina said, and we all kept walking. Leigh didn't say another word.

"Hey, Starbuck, how's your dad?" Regina asked.

"Not good," I said. Then, because I didn't want to sound mean, I added, "But thank you for asking."

And then we were at the office. I had never been in trouble like this before, so I was pretty hesitant about entering, but Regina banged the door open and announced, "Mr. Thompson called us down."

"What'd you do this time, Regina?" one of the secretaries said in an oddly friendly voice.

"Mayhem, destruction, you know."

"Why? What was your reason this time?"

"It was Mayhem Monday. I kinda had a theme going on."

The secretary half laughed and half sighed. "I'll let him know you're here. But I really wish you'd start controlling your temper. You're such a smart girl."

After the secretary got up and turned her back, Regina rolled her eyes. But I think she was secretly pleased, because she wasn't scowling like she usually did after adults talked to her. Ryder smiled at her, and she said, "What? Shut up! She's friends with my mom at church!"

"What?" Ryder asked, looking innocent. "I didn't say anything. I really wish you'd start controlling your temper. You're such a—uh-oh."

Mrs. Selinsky came out of the principal's office and walked past us, smirking. Then the secretary stepped into the doorway and gestured for the five of us to come and sit in a conference room. It looked like a police interrogation chamber from a bad movie. There was absolutely nothing in there aside from the table and chairs, although there was a plain tin bowl full of miniature candy canes in the middle of the tabletop. It was like, "Happy holidays from all of us at youaredoomed.com!"

As soon as we had gotten in there and seated ourselves, the principal appeared in the doorway. I wasn't
sure what to do—were we supposed to stand back up?
I mean, it's not like he was the American flag or anything,
but he was the boss of us.

I decided that sucking up was a good career move—
not that I cared—so I stood partway up. Christopher and
Leigh did, too. Regina stayed in her seat, and Ryder started
to stand, then stopped awkwardly halfway up. Ryder was
always so cocky. If even he was unsure of himself in front
of Mr. Thompson, I figured there was about a fifty percent
chance I would say or do something incredibly dumb or
embarrassing. Or, you know, get myself kicked out of
middle school and end up working the garbage-bin detail
at McDonald's the rest of my life.

"So," the principal said in a surprisingly cheerful voice,
"we all had a bit of a scare yesterday. Maybe things got a
little heated, maybe people said some things they might
regret now that things have calmed down a bit. Personally,
I'm just glad we're all safe. Anyone want a candy cane?"

Then he actually pushed the bowl of candy canes
around the table to each of us. I took one—even though
my orthodontist would have killed me—because my
orthodontist was way across town, wasn't about to

interrogate me, and didn't hold life-or-death power over my cell phone at the moment.

Next, he sat back, laced his fingers over the middle of his belly, and said, "So. Tell me about this misunderstanding in your science classroom yesterday."

First, Leigh said, "I don't know anything. I was just sitting there filing my nails the whole time."

"Really?" Mr. Thompson asked.

"Really."

"That's interesting, because the lockdown lasted over an hour. You'd think your fingers would be filed down to about the second knuckle by now. Not to mention the difficulty of doing manicure work in the dark. Hmm. Let's hear from someone else. You're Christopher, right?"

Christopher said, "Yes."

"Can you tell me what happened yesterday?"

"Yes, I can," Christopher said. Then he just sat there.

Mr. Thompson sighed. "Christopher," he said, "please tell me what happened yesterday."

"All right. I woke up at seven nineteen a.m. I knew it would be a bad day then, because seven and nineteen are both prime numbers. Then I got up and went into the bathroom. I splashed water on my face, because my eyes felt somewhat crusty and—"

"Christopher," Mr. Thompson said, "please tell me what happened in science class yesterday after the lights went off. I am especially interested in what was said between your group and Mrs. Selinsky."

"I was patting Claire. Claire is my friend. She is nice to me. Other children are not always nice to me. Claire was crying, because her father is in the hospital. Her brother kept sending her texts about his condition, and that made Mrs. Selinsky yell. Mrs. Selinsky said, 'Phone. Now.' Then Ryder said, 'You don't understand. This is a real emergency. Please don't take Claire's phone. Her father is in the emergency room. He's about to go into surgery.' But Mrs. Selinsky said, 'Rules are rules.' I did not understand why she said that, because of course rules are rules. What else would rules be? They are not cats or cheeses."

Mr. Thompson sighed again, then said, "Continue."

"Ryder said, 'Take my phone instead of Claire's,' or something like that. I was not exactly sure, because I was still trying to understand that part about rules are rules. Then he asked Mrs. Selinsky how she would have liked it if a teacher had taken away Meredith's phone in an emergency. Meredith is Mrs. Selinsky's daughter. My mother says Mrs. Selinsky should stop blabbing about her daughter and start teaching us some science. Then Mrs. Selinsky said, 'How DARE you bring up my daughter to me? Don't you ever mention her name again.' I was frightened, because Mrs. Selinsky looked like the Grinch. The Grinch makes me cry. When I was little, I used to wet my pants when he came on the television screen, but then my mother explained that he was just a character. Mrs. Selinsky is scarier, because she is real."

"And then?"

A shadow fell over the table. Mrs. Selinsky had appeared in the doorway. I wondered whether she had been standing outside for a while, listening.

"Then Claire's phone lit up again. And Mrs. Selinsky took it. And Claire reached out. And Mrs. Selinsky slapped her. Teachers are not supposed to slap students. That is a rule!"

"And then?"

"And then Regina Chavez yelled, 'Hey, give her the phone back, you crazy BEEP!'" Like Regina, Christopher didn't really say BEEP.

Everybody sat there in total silence for long enough that I could hear Christopher panting. He sounded almost as bad as my father. I wanted to reach out and touch his hand, but I was afraid that might make him scream. I had never realized how terrified he must have been at school, so much of the time.

Finally, Mr. Thompson turned to me, and said, "Claire, is this true?"

"Yes," I said. "It's true. Mrs. Selinsky *is* a crazy BEEP."

But I didn't actually say BEEP, either.

20. To Be Fair, I Do Figure Things Out Eventually

"Young lady, do you understand the seriousness of this situation?" Mr. Thompson asked.

I had a moment of incredible, skin-prickling panic.

Then Leigh, who had sat through this entire meeting like a statue with her arms crossed, suddenly leaned forward and interjected, "Sir, would you say Claire's situation is more or less serious than Mrs. Selinsky's? I mean, we're talking about a kid who said a bad word, versus a teacher who went crazy screaming and yelling during a supposedly silent shelter-in-place emergency, and then smacked a child in front of a roomful of witnesses. I'm no lawyer, but I'd have to bet Mrs. S is actually in more trouble than Claire is. If I were the two of you, I'd give back Claire's phone, let us all go back to class right now, and never say another thing about this. By the way, I said I'm no lawyer, but do you know who *is*? My father. So anyway, those are *my* thoughts."

"Well, umm . . . Mrs. Selinsky, what are your thoughts? Maybe we could all sit down and come to some kind of agreement. Perhaps a behavioral contract for these students, in exchange for not putting any consequences in place right now?"

Mrs. Selinsky nodded, very slightly. She looked like she wanted to choke each of us, though.

Slowly.

"But wait," Regina said. "This lady slapped Claire. Now she's just going to get away with it?"

Mr. Thompson's fists clenched, and for a moment, it appeared we might see another round of student abuse, but then he relaxed his hands and said, "Mrs. Selinsky, will you excuse us for a moment? I just want to have a private chat with these students about their attitudes. Then maybe their behavior in your class will turn in a positive direction."

"But—"

"Please trust me."

Mrs. Selinsky stormed out, and Mr. Thompson let all the air out of his lungs with a huge, whistling sigh. "You know, kids, that woman has been on the faculty of this school since I was a student here. She opened this building thirty-two years ago. She won the very first Teacher of the Year award here, and she's won the most awards of any educator in the history of the school. When she retires at the end of this year, I will be far from the only person crying at the dinner.

"Now, I know what you're going to say, because I have heard it all before from other students and parents over the past two years. 'She yells at us! She isn't nice! She's scary! She's always comparing us to her perfect daughter, Meredith!'"

I looked around the table, and everybody was leaning forward and nodding. This was weird. It was like a teacher was telling us the truth.

"But here's the part you *don't* know. Meredith really was a pretty amazing girl. She was in my graduating class. Oh, we all loved her. She did everything well—she was the drum major in marching band, the captain of the girls' tennis team, homecoming queen, third in our class. And so kind and thoughtful.

"Meredith went away to college, and had some stupid argument with her mother about curfew while she was home on break. One thing led to another, and they stopped speaking. Meredith never came home again. Oh, it broke her mother's heart. Mrs. Selinsky never let any of that affect her work here, though. She kept track of Meredith's life from a distance—I think she always hoped for a second chance. I know Meredith got married, got divorced, got remarried—and then, two and a half years ago, she was diagnosed with liver cancer."

Now we were all leaning super-far forward, with our

bottom jaws hanging down. It must have looked like we were waiting for Mr. Thompson to start throwing pop-corn into our mouths.

"So then what happened?" Ryder asked.

"Then she died."

"Did Mrs. Selinsky get to say good-bye?" I asked.

Mr. Thompson raised an eyebrow. "You've been in her class all year. What do you think?"

"Umm, no?"

"Umm, no. So maybe now you might be a little bit more understanding of Mrs. Selinsky's . . . temperament. Her situation isn't the easiest. So no, she shouldn't have yelled at you, and she probably went a little overboard with the phones. And she definitely should not have hit your hand, Claire—if that is indeed what she meant to do. But it also sounds as though a few of you might do well to check your attitudes at the door. Do you think you can do that? I would consider it a personal favor. And I never forget a personal favor.

"Now. Leigh?"

"I didn't even do anything!"

"Leigh!"

"Yeah, I guess so."

"Thank you. Regina?"

"Yes."

"Claire?"

"Yes. And may I please have my phone back? I really do need it, because my father really *is* in the hospital."

"We can make that happen. Give me a couple of periods. Now the rest of you can go. I just need another moment with Claire."

The other four got out of there so fast, it was like the seats had an ejector function.

Then I sat there, trying hard not to bite my nails. It was the first time I had ever been alone in a room with a principal before. He was really big. And kind of hairy. Plus, his toupee was hideous. The situation was awkward in the extreme.

"Claire," he said finally.

"Yes, Mr. Thompson?"

"You aren't going to use language like that in my building anymore, are you?"

"No, sir."

"Good. Now, about your father. Is there anything we can do to make your life easier right now? Would it help if your teachers got your assignments together ahead of time in case things suddenly come up at home? Or would you like the counselor to check in on you?"

"No, thank you."

"You know, I read two of your dad's books with my younger son. I cried like a baby when the hamster died in *Cat in the Box*. I'm really sorry for what you and your family must be going through."

"Uh, I appreciate that."

"Just please try to remember that we in this school are a family, too. We're here to help each other out, okay?"

I nodded, and he sent me back to class.

Regina was waiting for me in the hall. "Hey, Starbuck, are you going to die?"

"Nah, they're letting me live."

"That's good," she said, with an odd look on her face. "I don't know how Ryder would survive if he didn't have you around."

"Uh, yeah. Well. Thanks for waiting for me."

"Thanks for having my back in there."

"Thanks for trying to get between me and Selinsky yesterday."

"Starbuck, sometimes you are so dumb. I didn't do that for *you*."

And it hit me: Mrs. Selinsky had been about to take her anger out on Ryder right before Regina stepped in. "You did it for Ryder."

"You're a little slow, but you got there eventually."

"Wow, you really like him."

"Ah, shut up."

"No, I'm not making fun of you. I'm serious."

"Well, then, yeah. But he likes *you*, Starbuck."

"Are you crazy? He's hated me since, like, the third day of band camp in sixth grade. He follows me around everywhere I go just so he can make my life miserable. He never leaves me alone. He—oh."

"Yeah. Oh."

"But I don't like him. No offense or anything. I don't mean I don't like him. I mean I don't *like* like him. I just . . . back in sixth grade I just wanted to stay friends with him. And then, all of a sudden, he woke up one day hating me. I don't suppose you have any idea why?"

Regina started walking down the hall. Over her shoulder, she said, "Why don't you ask him?"

"Okay, I will!"

"Good!"

"Okay, then!"

Just before she turned the corner and disappeared, she said, "By the way, don't think this makes us friends or anything, Starbuck!"

Which was a relief. It was bad enough finding out that Mrs. Selinsky and my school principal were both secretly human. Becoming friends with Regina on the same day might have snapped my mind completely.

I stopped at the bathroom to splash some water on my face. Mostly, I just needed the time alone, though. When I walked in, I was relieved to see there was nobody at the sinks. The water felt good and cold against my skin, a feeling that was worth the disgusting smell of the school paper towels. As I was patting my face dry, Leigh sort of exploded out of the corner stall, causing the metal door to bang against the wall tiles. I felt like I jumped about a foot, which made Leigh smile.

But when I looked at her face, her ever-present makeup was smudged, as though she had been crying. I only got a quick glimpse, though, because she immediately wet a paper towel and started scrubbing violently at her eye area.

Well, this was awkward. On the one hand, she was, like, the evil spider girl at the center of my school's web of cruelty and mockery. On the other, she had just stood up for me with the principal. I stood there like a moron, try-ing to think of something semi-friendly to say that she couldn't throw back in my face immediately or use against me later.

But faster than you can say, "Hey, I love your boots," Leigh's eyes flashed in my direction. She grinned as though everything was perfectly normal, and said, "Well, that was fun. Did you see the look on Selinsky's *face* when I said my dad was a *lawyer?* Wow. Good times."

Then she grabbed a wad of dry paper towels, patted her face with them, and strode past me as she flung them over her shoulder in the general direction of the trash can. She missed by about a foot and a half, but by the time the towels hit the floor, the bathroom door was already swinging shut behind her.

I would almost have believed her "good times" act, except that she had just walked out into a public space without makeup. Leigh without makeup was like a math teacher without a calculator, a Disney princess without huge eyes, a knight without shining armor.

A viper without fangs.

I didn't have the time or energy to stand there and analyze Leigh's issues, though, because (A) I was now ten minutes later than the time on my hall pass, and (B) Leigh was pretty far down my list of people to worry about.

At lunch, two remarkable things happened. First, Mr. Thompson came out of nowhere, reached over my shoulder, and gently placed my phone on the table in front of me, between my PB&J and my vanilla milk. I was like, *Wow. That was fast. Also, I had no idea this man knew where the cafeteria was.*

"Thank you, Mr. Thompson," I managed to stammer.

"You're welcome. Now, Claire, remember what we talked about, okay?"

"Okay."

"I'm serious."

"Okay."

"*Remember,*" he said again, in this spooky "Use the Force, Luke" kind of dramatic whisper. Then he winked and started to turn away. I was like, *Blech! The principal just winked at me. Does he think we're bonding now?*

Regina said, "Wait, Mr. Thompson! You want some Skittles?"

He did. She poured, like, half the pack into his hand.

"Thanks! I love these!" he exclaimed in a burst of refreshingly fruit-flavored joy.

"Absolutely no problem, sir. 'Cause they're Star—uh, Claire's."

"I kind of like you, Chavez," Mr. Thompson said. "I'm going to be watching you and your friends like a hawk from now until June, but still. I admire your spunk."

After he walked away, Ryder said, "I admire your spunk!" and then cracked up.

"*Remember,*" Regina replied, before bursting into giggles herself.

"What just happened?" Roshni asked. "Am I crazy, or did our principal just walk up to our lunch table and hand deliver your phone to you?"

"Um, both?" Ryder said.

Roshni shot a rude gesture in his direction.

"Uh, our meeting in the office was pretty . . . um . . . interesting. A lot of stuff happened. And now, I guess, well, Mr. Thompson told us some things, sooooo . . ."

Regina waved her hand to cut me off. "What Starbuck is trying to say is that T and us are tight now."

Roshni said, "Huh. How 'bout Christopher and Leigh?"

"Nah, they ain't tight. That's all right, though. I don't think Christopher is really looking for a relationship right now."

"Ha-ha."

"Christopher was never in trouble in the first place," I said. "I think he was more of a witness. Leigh wasn't exactly in trouble at first, but then she went off on Mrs. Selinsky. It was kind of rude and also kind of awesome."

"Aw, you *know* I hate that girl," Regina said, "but it was *crazy* awesome. She was like, 'Don't even *make* me bring my lawyer army down here.'"

"Yeah," I said, "that's pretty much how it went."

"So what's supposed to happen with Mrs. Selinsky now?"

"We're going to be nice to her," I said.

"WHAT? After what she did yesterday? After what she's done all year?"

"Woman's been through some stuff," Regina said.

"I'm serious," Ryder said.

"And, hey, June's still six months away. A truce might be kind of nice, right? I know I could use some peace and quiet in my life," I added.

Just then the table rattled and my phone lit up.

21. Breaking Through, Breaking Down

The text from my mom was very simple:

Your father is talking!!!

I wrote back:

You mean he's breathing better and saying some words?

Her next message said:

I mean he is talking. The doctors think it might be an effect of the oxygen, or maybe the steroids he is on unswelled something in his brain. Anyway, really talking. Sentences. Grandma is coming to get you.

I could practically hear her crying through the phone. I looked up from the screen, and found my whole table staring at me.

"Well?" Roshni said. "Are you okay? Is everything all right? Because I know pneumonia can be a disaster. And my mother said a lot of the common antibiotics aren't working anymore because of resistant bacteria. Not that your father's pneumonia is necessarily a disaster. And he might not have a resistant infection. He could be just fine. I mean, forget I said anything. Just go ahead with your story."

I swear, I love the girl, but I might have to start carrying around a roll of duct tape so I can slap a strip across her mouth when she gets nervous and starts babbling.

"He's fine," I said. "At least, I think he is. In fact, he just started talking in sentences for the first time since September."

"Maybe he could take some of *your* extra sentences, Roshni," Regina said. "Then you could talk a normal amount, and everybody would be happy."

That Regina really knows how to sweeten a moment, doesn't she?

. . . .

You can't imagine what that night was like. Dad was still kind of sick, and very weak. Still, his color was better, he wasn't sweating all over the place, and his fever had broken, so those were all great signs, apparently. Mom told me that the oxygen tube clipped to his nose had been turned down so that it was pumping only something like half as much per minute as he had needed the day before, and his feeding tube was gone.

But of course, the biggest deal was the talking. When I first walked into the room, I was almost afraid to say any-thing, because it seemed too good to be true. I kind of tiptoed in, and then edged my way along the wall until I was next to my mom. She squeezed my hand and smiled at me.

Then Dad looked up at me, and both of his eyes were completely locked in on mine. I can't really explain it, but I felt like he was really *there* again. "Claire," he said.

I went to him, put my head on his chest, and cried like a baby.

"Oh, my Claire. You . . . saved . . . me."

. . . .

Two days after that, Dad came home. He had gained three pounds in the hospital, which was apparently an exciting development. We had strict orders to keep filling him up with food, and to follow a new exercise plan that came complete with weights and workout equipment in our basement.

Unfortunately, his good mood didn't survive the short journey across town.

He didn't want to eat. He didn't want to exercise. He didn't want to work with his therapists (although at least I continued to miss most of that action because it happened while I was at school). All he kept saying over and over was "Let me sleep."

Mom said that maybe he had been wanting to say it for months, and now he needed to get it all out before he could get back to being his old self. That was typical Mom: "Look on the bright side! He's saying completely miserable stuff over and over, but at least he's talking!"

Matthew just muttered curses and left the room whenever the complaining started. Matthew had always been Mr. Go-Go-Go. If he had to study, he studied a million times harder than everybody else. If he was going to train for a sport, he was on the field until they turned the lights off and yelled at him to go home. The same with trumpet. I remember when I was little and he first got his horn for Hanukkah. The next morning, he'd played the C scale over and over—through breakfast time, through lunchtime, through dinner—until our parents took the instrument away for the night.

It must have driven him crazy to see our dad acting like a quitter.

As for me, I didn't know how to handle it. All I knew was that my father had been the one person in the family who was most likely to make me smile, but now if I heard him say, "Leave me alone, I'm tired," one more time, I was going to smash my head through a wall.

. . . .

At my last private dance lesson before Christmas break, Miss Laura was in an extra-good mood. Three younger girls had just come in and given her candy and cookies, and she was tapping one foot and humming along with the warm-up music while I did my stretches. I guess that's why I decided to shoot my stupid mouth off. "Miss Laura," I said, "is there any chance I might *ever* move up into the advanced classes with my friends? I mean, I'm still really hoping there might be."

Her foot stopped tapping so suddenly, it was as if she'd just stepped on a nail. Actually, the look on her face was what you might expect from somebody whose foot had just been impaled. "Well, do you think you *deserve* to get moved up?"

Eek. "I don't know. I've been taking privates with you since September, and I do my core exercises at home. Plus, I try hard in my classes, I think."

Miss Laura stood there for the longest time and stared me down while I attempted to figure out what to do with myself. Was I supposed to keep stretching? Stop stretching and bow down before her? Run out of the room and try to find a crowbar for her foot?

When she spoke, I immediately felt nostalgia for the good old days of standing around like a moron. "Claire," she hissed, "here's a hint. If your answer to whether you deserve to get moved up starts with 'I don't know,' you probably aren't going to get moved up."

"But—"

"Honey, I know you've been through a lot this year, with your father and everything. And I know it's hard when your friends move up without you. But here's the thing: Your friends are better dancers than you are. Remember when you all used to giggle and mess around at the barre, and your teachers used to tell you to pay attention? At some point, those girls figured it out and you didn't. Sooner or later, what you do or don't do at the barre shows up out on the floor."

"But I'm trying so hard *now*."

"That's great, but some of the girls in the next level have been trying hard since they were five years old. They take more classes than you do. A few of them have amazing natural talent, but basically it just comes down to work. How hard are you going to work? If you work really, really super hard from now until June, we're still not talking about moving up in the middle of this year—but you might have a shot at being in your friends' classes in the fall."

My eyes were burning, but I didn't want Miss Laura to have the satisfaction of seeing tears roll down my face. I turned away from her, and pretended I'd developed a sudden fascination for the dorky ballerina clock in the far back corner of the room.

"Claire," she said, "you can cry, or you can hold it in. But either way, the only way you're going to get what you want is to bust your butt until the dancer you *are* is the dancer you *need to be*. Now wipe your face and let's see some of the combinations we were working on last week. And keep your shoulders back. You look all shlumpy."

Great. In the lovely world of Dance Expressions, it's okay to be depressed, abused, and heartbroken. But you'd better not be shlumpy.

. . . .

Over the break, I have to admit I came really close to just quitting dance altogether. I think the only reason I stayed was to prove Miss Nina and Miss Laura were wrong about me. I wanted to show everybody I didn't deserve to be in the Puberty 101 classes. So yeah, hooray for bitterness, the Great and Noble Motivator.

I wasn't the only bitter member of my family. Matthew

was stomping and fuming his way through the holiday season like a junior version of Ebenezer Scrooge. We celebrate Hanukkah, because Dad was raised Jewish, and Christmas, because Mom was raised Catholic. Hanukkah was sad enough, because Dad had always been the one who lit the candles, and this year his hand wasn't steady enough. But Christmas was worse.

The night before Christmas, in the middle of decorating the tree, Mom was getting all nostalgic like she always does, telling the story behind each ornament, getting all misty-eyed about the ones Matthew and I had made when we were little. Dad was struggling to help by attaching hooks to the ornaments, which I guess must be pretty hard when you're right-handed but your right hand is shaky and weak. I was doing my best to act like everything was fine, for Mom and Dad. But Matthew was just tapping his foot, sighing, looking at his phone over and over, and gazing longingly at the stairs that lead up to our rooms.

Finally, not even Mom—who is basically the most relentlessly fake-cheerful person I know when she sets her mind to it—could ignore the blatant disrespect. I mean, personally, I would probably have cracked about fifteen minutes before she did. Anyway, she said, "What is it, Matthew? What do you want? What is so important that it can't wait until we are done decorating our tree?"

"What do I want? I want to go upstairs and study."

"Oh, Matthew, who studies on Christmas Eve?"

"*I* do. Look, do you know what I want for Christmas, Mom? I want my soccer season back. I want my girlfriend back. I want my *life* back. But since I can't get any of those things, I thought it might be nice if I could at least salvage my grades, or possibly pull out some half-decent SAT scores."

Dad looked up at Matthew. "You . . . didn't play . . . ball?" he asked.

"Uh, no, Dad."

"Because of . . . my head?"

"Well, yeah. But it wasn't your fault or anything. I'm not blaming you, I swear. It's just something that happened. I'm not mad at you. I'm just mad. Oh, God. I'm sorry. Crap!" Matthew sat down on the couch next to our father.

I was shocked. Matthew never said even the mildest bad word. For him to say "Crap," he had to be right at the edge of a breakdown, leaning out and possibly kicking a few pebbles over the side.

"Me, too," Dad said. "I am too mad."

"So . . . who's up for some eggnog?" Mom asked.

. . . .

Dad's therapy exercises were brutal. He had to balance on his weak foot atop a weird rubberized half globe; do all sorts of small, intricate movements with string, using his weak hand; lift weights; stretch his weak side for long periods of time; and even do modified versions of push-ups and sit-ups. The therapists said he had to work on his tone, flexibility, and control. Every time he complained about the work, Mom would say those three words over and over to him: *Tone, flexibility, control.*

Dad would reply, "Sleep. Sleep. Sleep."

So one day, when he was down in the basement, sitting in the middle of all the equipment, I tried to make him a deal. I started to explain about my dance problems, but he cut me off, and said, "I know about your . . . dance . . . thing. I couldn't talk, but I was not . . . the thing when you can't hear."

"Deaf."

"Deaf. I was not deaf."

"Well, anyway, I want to get better, and you need to work out. I'm off for the next ten days. Why don't we work out together? Maybe it will make us both work harder."

"I don't *want* to work harder. Working harder is . . . not sharp. Untippy. Unpointy."

"Pointless?"

"Yes! Pointless. I get tired, and at the end, I am still slow . . . and weak."

"But it's not pointless, Dad! I mean, if you don't get in shape, you're going to look kind of silly when it's time for the Dads' Dance."

"What?"

"The Dads' Dance. At Expressions. You know? I'm going to be fourteen this year. It's time for us to dance together."

"Claire, I can't dance. I can't even walk right. I can barely stay . . . not asleep."

"Awake."

"I can barely stay . . . awake."

I had assumed for months there was no way he would be able to do the Dads' Dance, but then when he'd started talking better, I had allowed myself a shred of hope. Stupid.

"You're right, Dad," I said. "Why don't you just sit and rest? I'll work out. I have to do the recital anyway, whether you're in it or not."

I ignored him for a while then, and worked on my splits until I could put one foot up on the first step of the stairs and still get my butt all the way down to the floor. The move was called an oversplit, and it was a new skill for me. The year before, I hadn't even been able to do a split consistently.

Next, I did planks and squats until my calves, arms, and thigh muscles were trembling and the sweat was starting to run down the back of my neck. At that point, I figured I was loose enough to practice some turns. Our basement isn't really big enough for major dance practice, and the addition of Dad's equipment hadn't helped, but I had just the right amount of space for a turn or two if I was careful not to get too crazy with my arm extension.

Oh, and the ceiling is low, so forget about those hands-over-head ballerina swan moves. But I could leap if I remembered to keep my arms down.

Whatever. My house was what it was, and the low ceiling was the least of my problems. I did what I could with what I had, while pointedly ignoring my father. I thought that maybe if he saw how hard I was working, he might be inspired to join in and start his workout.

Then he would get hungry, eat a ton of nourishing food, gain lots of healthy weight, get all better, never have to go back to the hospital, start writing again . . . my pliés, relevés, and tendus would save our family! And I would be the greatest dancer ever! Miss Nina would cry at my feet and beg forgiveness! But I would laugh and step over her quivering body, gracefully kicking her in the teeth as I bent over to gather up the flowers thrown to me by my adoring fans! And—

My fantasy was interrupted by a buzz-saw sound behind me. Dad was slumped over on his special stroke-patient yoga mat, snoring.

The next day, though, when I said I was going downstairs to work out, he followed. I started stretching my hamstrings, and he stood on the odd half-globe ball. I switched to squats, and he moved over to his knot-tying toys. Halfway through my planks, I noticed he was still bent over a big plastic board with strings attached to it, mumbling and cursing.

"Dad, do you need help?" I asked.

"No," he said. "If you help me, I'll never get my knot-tying . . . merit . . . badge."

"Wow, did you just make a joke?"

"I might have."

I jumped up and hugged him. "Dad," I said, "that's the first time you've made a joke since September!"

"Well, it has not been a very funny time."

"Yeah, but I missed you."

"I missed me, too."

I squeezed his neck.

"But," he said, "don't think this means I'm ready to go on the . . . place where everybody watches you."

"The stage."

"Yeah. Don't think I'm ready to go on the stage. I can't even tie a shoelace knot. And my joke wasn't that good."

"I think it was amazing, Daddy."

My father shrugged my arms off from around his shoulders, and said, "Okay, enough for one day. Tired."

"Okay, but this was a good first day together. Think positive thoughts. Miss Amy at dance always says, 'If your thoughts are light, your feet will be light.'"

"Well, maybe my . . . left foot will be light, at least."

Two jokes in one day. It was a start.

22. An Interesting Definition

Things were pretty strange in science for a while after break. Mrs. Selinsky went out of her way to be super-duper normal. She didn't scream and yell, she didn't rant about Meredith, she didn't even jump onto any desks. It was like she had been warned to be on her best behavior.

Truthfully, class was kind of boring.

I felt sort of guilty about the whole thing. Mrs. S had been really mean, but so had we. And then, once I found out about her terrible secret, all I could picture was her going home alone every night to an empty house and crying herself to sleep. I had no idea whether there was a Mr. Selinsky around, but if there was, she never mentioned him, and he didn't seem to be doing a very amazing job of keeping his wife happy.

So one day, I stayed behind after everyone else left. We had taken a quiz, and Mrs. S was packing up all the papers into her bag as I approached her desk. When she looked up and saw me standing there, she looked hostile for a split second, but then her eyes just became kind of neutral.

That was almost worse.

"May I help you?" she asked.

"Umm . . . I just wanted to say I'm sorry. For what I said about you in the principal's office."

She looked at me for a long time, and then said, "Thank you. But you were right. I *was* being . . . Well, I'm just going to say you were right."

Wow, there's something you don't hear every day, I thought.

"Don't get me wrong. Your class had gotten out of control, but that was my fault, too. When I was a young teacher, just starting out, my department supervisor told me, 'Never forget that *you* control the weather in your classroom.' She was right, but I forgot, and let a little storm develop.

"Anyway, it's over. I'm sorry for my part, and you're sorry for yours. Let's just move on."

"Uh, okay," I said, but I wasn't sure whether we were done talking. Mrs. Selinsky might have been in "sane" mode, but I still couldn't figure her out. Everything she did was always kind of jerky and sudden.

"You can go now, by the way."

I opened my mouth to say something else, then lifted a hand to wave, then just settled on turning and starting to walk out of the room. *Smooth*, I thought.

"Oh, there is one other thing, actually."

I turned back around in the doorway.

"I hope you appreciate how lucky you are to have the friends you do."

"Oh, you mean the kids in my group? They're not really my friends. Actually, we don't even get along a lot of the time."

"I don't care about that. Look, Clarise—"

"Um, it's Claire."

"Look, Claire, each of those children deliberately stood between you and me. And I'm a pretty frightening teacher, if you stop and think about it. Anyone who would do that certainly sounds like a friend to me."

. . . .

Ryder was waiting for me by the lockers. "Hey, Claire," he said. "Chair auditions for jazz band are coming up. If you want, I could ask Mrs. Jones to postpone them for the saxes so you have more time to get ready. I mean, I don't mind or anything. Your mom told mine how you've been spending all your extra time helping your dad, soooo . . ."

Oh my God, I thought. *Ryder is being openly nice to me. Is this yet another psychological trick? Or could it be that Mrs. Selinsky was right about this friend thing? Because if so, that's kind of disturbing.*

I felt my old instinctive anger start to well up. "For your information, Ryder, I've been practicing. I've been playing the sax for my father, like, daily for weeks now. He enjoys my playing. I'm not some pathetic charity case who needs special favors from—"

That was when I noticed. Ryder had been smiling at me—not grinning or sneering maliciously, but actually smiling. And now his smile was fading fast.

What am I doing? I thought.

"Hold on, Ryder. I'm sorry. I didn't mean to jump on you. I just have a lot going on right now."

"I know."

My mind flashed on the things Regina had said to me after the meeting with Mr. Thompson. "Can I ask you something? Why did you stop being friends with me in sixth grade? I mean, we used to laugh together all the time in elementary school, and then all of a sudden, we got here and BAM! You suddenly decided you were too cool for me."

Ryder's face turned red. "That's not what happened at all."

"Well, that's how it seemed to me."

Ryder looked down at the floor, and exhaled slowly. Then he breathed in and, still without looking at me, said, "No. It was the third day of band camp. The band moms were measuring us for our uniforms. You had already gone, so you were standing around talking to Roshni and Jennifer when it was my turn. The lady measured my height, and then my arms and legs. Okay, whatever. But when she did my waist, she started muttering and looking at the papers she had—I don't know, the lists of uniforms in stock or something. And then she shouted out across the whole cafeteria, 'Hey, Liz, we're gonna need some extra fabric for this kid's pants!'"

That sounded pretty traumatic. But I didn't see what it had to do with me.

Ryder looked up from the floor and locked eyes with me. "You don't even remember this, do you?"

I shook my head.

"You *giggled*, Claire. You and Roshni and Jennifer. You all covered your mouths like you weren't laughing, but you were. And I just had to stand there like a fat little dork while two other moms came over and had some stupid band-uniform crisis conference right in front of everyone. I just wanted to *die*. That's when I stopped being your friend. When *you* stopped being mine."

Tears sprang up at the corners of my eyes as suddenly as though somebody had just slapped my nose. It was weird—I had never been much of a crier until eighth grade, but since September, I had been weeping out of control at the slightest little disturbance.

It's amazing what nonstop trauma will do to a person.

Anyway, I reached out and took Ryder's hand. "I'm sorry, Ryder. I'm sorry it happened to you, I'm sorry I laughed, and I'm sorry I don't remember it. That must have been terrible."

He looked down at our hands in shock. I was afraid for a moment that he might faint. His face had already been pretty flushed, but now it looked like someone had rubbed cherry juice all over him or something.

Finally, he started giggling. It was so bizarre and unexpected that I did, too. The giggles built into a wave of laughter, which crested and built again into another one. We didn't get ourselves back under control until I was out of breath and Ryder was wheezing like a leaky balloon.

Then he gasped, "Ah, it wasn't that bad. At least I got a custom-made band uniform out of the deal. The fit was snug, yet breezy. So, do you want the extra time before auditions, or what?"

"No," I said, and I could feel a real, honest, happy smile pulling up at the sides of my mouth. "I want to kick your butt fair and square."

"Wait a minute, Storky. You think you're going to kick my butt? You and what secret woodwind army?"

"Ryder, you have not yet begun to appreciate my reedy wrath. Prepare for total saxophonical devastation. I'm talking epic, massive alto obliteration."

"From you? Please."

Three weeks later, when auditions rolled around, I got second chair. Ryder got first. I said, "Congratulations."

Ryder replied, "In your face!" But he was smiling when he said it.

23. Schooling and Getting Schooled

"Fish! Spit! Fit! Shiff!"

Dad was throwing his hand-exercise balls all over the basement, shouting nonsense words, when I walked downstairs. When he noticed my presence, he said, "Claire, help me!"

"Sure," I said, starting to pick up the balls. "What can I do?"

"Don't give me back the . . . silver torture things! Jesus. Just tell me the word. I just can't think of what you say when . . . you're throwing stuff and yelling. It sounds like 'pit' or 'ship' or something, but I can't get it. It's right on the tip of my . . . mouth thing. It's driving me crazy. I can't just toss stuff around and scream, 'Slip!' all the time. That's not . . . satisfying."

I was like, *Dude, can't you just learn your curses from the other kids on the kindergarten bus like a normal person?* But obviously, that wasn't an option. So I said, "Okay, Dad. Here's the deal. I'll teach you the word if you get through your whole workout today without quitting on me."

He thought about it for a while, and then said, "Deal."

We almost made it, too, but then three-quarters of the way through, Dad slipped off his balance ball and fell over onto the carpet. "I *hate* that stupid thing!" he barked. "I hate all of this. I can't get through my exercises without screwing up."

"Well, Dad, you know what Miss Laura says when I feel sorry for myself at dance?"

"What?"

"You can cry or you can hold it in. But either way, the only way you're going to get what you want is to bust your butt until the dancer you *are* is the dancer you *need to be*."

"You know I'm not dancing in your show, right?"

I kept talking. "That's not the point, Dad. The point is that if you quit, you're just going to be a bitter old crippled guy. I don't care if you limp. I don't care if your hand shakes. But you're acting like you're broken inside, and that's not who you are. That's not who you were before. That's not MY DAD! Now please get up and get back on that ball."

He stared into my eyes for the longest time without saying a word, but I didn't look away. Eventually, he got back up, and balanced for maybe twenty seconds. Then he did the exercise again.

I felt like I'd been holding my breath for months without even realizing it, and now . . . just the slightest bit . . . I could start to exhale.

· ·

But I was still crushed that I didn't have a partner for the Dads' Dance. I slept over at Katherine's house one night during Easter break, which was right before the fathers were supposed to start rehearsing. Both Katherine's and Alanna's fathers offered to ask whether they could somehow do a double dance with me and their daughters. I told them I appreciated the gesture but that if I couldn't dance with my own father, I didn't see the point.

Mostly, I was just afraid I would be one of those embarrassing girls who breaks down and cries onstage while the whole audience sits and stares.

Katherine and Alanna were totally sympathetic, of course. Then we went upstairs, climbed into our sleeping bags, and ate junk food in the dark for hours. I loved just being there between the two of them, until Alanna asked me, "So, Claire, I don't mean to be bitchy or anything, but why have you been so distant lately? We haven't seen you outside of dance for months. You've been ignoring texts, which you never, ever used to do, and you're not talking to either of us about anything *real*. I mean, we all know you have a ton going on, but you know Katherine and I are here for you, right? We're supposed to be your besties. You can tell us stuff. You can trust us. You're not supposed to hide your problems. Unless it's something we did. Have we been rude? Have we been bugging you too much?"

Katherine said, "Is it because we didn't text you after your school lockdown? See, Alanna, I told you we should have texted her. Claire, Alanna was like, 'Give her space,' but I knew you'd want support. It was probably pretty traumatic, right? God, I'm so stupid."

"No, it has nothing to do with anything either of you did. Mostly, it's just been weird for me because . . ." And then I suddenly had to stop talking because I got all choked up.

Instantly, Alanna's arm encircled me from one side, and Katherine's hand was stroking my hair from the other. "Because what?" Alanna asked. "You can tell us anything."

"Because you were both in the high school classes, and I wasn't. I thought you were making new friends, and you wouldn't care about me anymore. I mean, not on purpose or anything, but . . . people drift apart all the time. And the high school girls' lives just always sound so glamorous and grown up when you talk about them. Meanwhile, I'm in, like, Training Bra Dance 101."

"Claire," Alanna said, "you're an idiot."

Ah, comforting, I thought.

"What kind of shallow dance drones do you think we are?" Katherine asked.

Alanna continued, "We're not your friends because of what class Miss Nina puts us in. We're your friends because we love you."

"Yeah," Katherine said. "You freaking bonehead."

. . . .

One day when I was getting set up to play sax for my father before dinner, my mother called me up to talk with her in the kitchen. "Claire," she said, "I don't know what you've been doing to motivate him, but it's been miraculous. Everybody is noticing: the physical therapist, the occupational therapist, the speech therapist. He's been taking walks around the block the past few mornings, by himself. That's a first. He's even starting to work on learning to read again. For a long time, he wouldn't even look at words on a page. Oh, honey! I just wanted to tell you how proud I am of you. I know we haven't gotten to spend much time together this year, and I haven't been telling you this from day to day, but you are doing an awesome job."

"Of what?"

She thought for a moment. "Of becoming *you*." Then she took me into her arms and gave me a bone-crushing hug. "So, there's something I've been meaning to discuss with you," she muttered into my hair. "I think I've found a partner for you for the Dads' Dance. I know it won't be the same as having your father up there, but still . . . I know this person wants to make the offer."

I pushed her away so I could look at her face. "Who are we talking about, Mom?"

Matthew stepped around the corner from the living room and said, "Yo."

"But—" I started to say.

"But what?" Matthew said.

"Well, you're not a dancer."

"Oh, and before this, Dad was secretly taking ballet lessons in an underground bunker?"

"No, but you . . . you don't have time. You've been having so much trouble managing everything as it is. You even had to dump your girlfriend. I can't ask you to do this. It's too much, Matthew."

"I don't know. Maybe I'll meet a hot junior at the rehearsals. This could be an extremely efficient use of my time."

"Oh, gross."

"No, seriously, I want to do this for you, Claire. And the big dress-rehearsal week is after school ends, right? So it won't be such a big deal. I'm taking my road test in a few weeks. We can drive to rehearsals together. Come on—it'll be excellent!"

I knew Matthew hated dancing, and I knew how much he guarded his time, so I knew what this offer meant to him. I nodded. "Okay," I said. "But you better take the rehearsals seriously. Dancing is hard."

"Oh, please," he said with a smirk. "How hard can it be? They let *you* in."

. . . .

At dinner one night in late spring, I said, "Hey, Dad, maybe you should write a book about this. I mean, you're working on reading and writing, right? That would give you a goal. And your story might really—I don't know—inspire people."

"Sure, Claire," he said, attempting to bring a spoonful of peas to his mouth and dropping several of them. "Who wouldn't want to be . . . like me?"

"No, I'm serious. Look how far you've come."

"Maybe. But maybe *you* should be the one to tell this story."

"Why me?" I asked.

"Because you and your brother are the . . . what do you call it? The heroes."

"Oh, come on, Dad."

236

"I'm serious. You could call it *The Drool Diaries*."

"Stop. Just stop."

"All right. The title needs . . . work. How about something simple, like *Piggy?*"

"Yuck."

"I'll keep working . . . on it."

The other thing he kept working on was losing his limp. He told me his physical therapist was so impressed by his progress with balance that he got a new exercise: stepping across the room by stomping down with the heel of one foot first, then whomping down forcefully with his toes, before doing the same with the other foot. It kind of looked like he was trying to be Frankenstein or a zombie or something, but he said it would strengthen his legs and improve his coordination.

I hadn't seen him work so hard on anything, so I didn't complain. But I really hoped he wasn't going to be walking like *that* in public.

Speaking of going out in public, one night after dinner, our mom had gone out to the grocery store. Dad suddenly turned to Matthew and said, "Let's go get . . . round . . . umm . . . donuts! Come on, Claire! We can surprise your . . . wife. No, your mother!"

I looked at Matthew, and he raised an eyebrow at me. We were both veterans of the dreaded Donut-Tossing

Massacre. On the other hand, this time, our father was *asking* to go. "Sure," Matthew said, exhaling slowly. "Let me just grab my car keys."

Dad ate three donuts that night, and didn't drop a single one. He did get rainbow sprinkles all over himself, but, hey—sprinkles are messy. That probably could have happened to anybody, right?

24. End of an Era

The last few weeks of middle school were incredibly weird. I don't know how many other people had this experience, but I found myself constantly turning to Roshni and saying, "So yeah. Apparently, *that* just happened."

The whole time, I felt a strange kind of doubleness, as if I was experiencing events while a separate part of me was floating overhead and watching them, detached. I can't explain it. Life was just super odd for a while. Mostly, I was blown away by the concept of leaving the place. I mean, all these things were happening in my head at once:

• I felt incredibly old. Like, *I am so one hundred percent ready for high school. In fact, they might as well just have me skip freshman year and give me sophomore status.*

• I felt like I was still the tiny pre–sixth grader who couldn't find the bathroom on the first day of band camp and accidentally opened a supply closet.

• I was going to miss everybody so, so much. I practically wanted to throw my arms around dear, sweet old Mrs. Selinsky.

• I was *so* done that I couldn't believe I still had to spend another four years with most of these fools.

• I wanted every second to be burned into my brain cells so I could replay it forever.

• I wanted to jump up from my desk and scream, *Let's go, already! Geez! If I have to watch another random movie, I'm going to Cabrillo myself right out the window!*

Plus, all the other kids were being bizarre. Regina came up to me at my locker on the way out of the building on the second-to-last day and handed me an envelope. I stood there for a minute staring at her, confused, until she said, "Uh, Starbuck, there's this thing some people do called The Opening of the Envelope."

So I tore it open, and a plastic rectangle fell out. It was a five-dollar gift card for Starbucks, with a Post-it note attached. The note said, *Payback for Skittles.*

I looked at her and smiled. "Did it ever occur to you that I might not even like Starbucks?"

"Oh, come on. You love it. I bet you a million bucks. Am I right?"

I couldn't help myself. I actually giggled out loud. "Oh, God, yes."

"Me, too. The pumpkin spice latte—I could drink that thing for days."

"Wow, Regina. That's a pretty girly drink. Do you get it with the whipped cream? Extra cinnamon? Some sugar substitute? A dash of nutmeg?"

"Oh, shut up."

"Regina likes a girly drink! Regina likes a girly drink!"

"You *know* I could still kill you with one finger, Starbuck."

"How can you still call me Starbuck when *you* love Starbucks?"

"'Cause it's still your name. Duh."

"Well, thanks for the card. And, uh, see you in high school."

Then I shocked myself by adding one more thing. "Maybe we'll have the same lunch. I'll bring the Skittles."

. . . .

I still had to go to the band room and bring home my sax for the last time, but as I turned the corner, I crashed into Ryder. He blushed furiously, and I realized that he must have been waiting for me.

I had never really thought about it before, but his crush was kind of sweet.

"What was that about?" he asked. His voice didn't have any of its usual sarcasm or fake casualness.

"What do you mean? Regina was just . . . well . . . she had something to give me."

"Did she, um, say anything?"

No, Ryder, when you're not around, we prefer to communicate through a complicated system of charades and mime.

"About what?"

Ryder's voice cracked. "About *me*."

Now my face got hot. *This is so awkward*, I thought. *He's afraid she told me about his brokenhearted, suffering love for me! It's kind of romantic, in a tragic way. How do I let him down gently? We've come so far. We're almost friends again. I can't ruin things now. What should I—*

"Because," he continued, "I'm going to ask her out tomorrow. I can't live all summer without knowing. It's bad enough I've been suffering through lunch for months like this."

Of course I did the single most disastrous thing in the world: I giggled.

"Again?" Ryder said. "Really? Again with the laughing? After all we've been through? How obnoxious are you?"

I held up my hand like a STOP sign while I tried to catch my breath. "Wait," I said. "I wasn't laughing at you. I was just laughing because—never mind. But you totally have a shot."

His face lit up. I had never seen him look so sincerely happy before. "I do? For real?" Then he frowned. "You'd better not be setting me up. Because this wouldn't be funny."

"Ryder, why do you think Regina sat at our lunch table all year when she didn't know Roshni and totally hated me?"

"Well, she doesn't hate you anymore. And she only hated you because I—never mind." He was blushing again.

"It doesn't matter. The point is, I have some inside info. Tell Regina how you feel."

Then Ryder grabbed me up in a huge bear hug that literally lifted my feet off the ground. When he put me down, he said, "Thank you." It sounded oddly formal coming from him.

I bowed and said, "You're welcome. By the way, I already told Regina this, but if you happen to be in my lunch next year, you're welcome to sit at my table. I'll bring the Skittles."

As he turned to walk away, he asked, "Since when is it *your* table?"

I smiled. There was the Ryder I knew.

. . . .

I was feeling daring on the last half day of my middle school career, so I wore fluorescent pink flip-flops, even though open-toed shoes are technically against our district dress code. All we were supposed to be doing all day was signing each other's yearbooks, and everyone knew grades were already in, so I didn't think the teachers were going to be cracking down too hard. Plus, I happen to love my fluorescent flops—they're my go-to footwear for the dance studio, and I never get the chance to wear them at school.

Leigh Monahan strutted in, late as usual, and her eyes immediately widened as they locked onto my feet. "I love your flip-flops, Claire!" she shouted from the doorway.

For a moment, my mind raced: Was she trying to get me in trouble by drawing attention to my contraband footwear? Was she being sarcastic, as in the Great Boot Disaster? Or was there—gasp!—a chance she actually liked my shoes? And then I realized that Leigh Monahan's opinion didn't really have any power over me anymore.

"Thanks," I said, and smiled at her.

She froze for a moment, then smiled back.

One of the two random boys in front of me turned to the other and said, "Something just happened, right?"

Roshni turned to me and rolled her eyes. "Boys!" she said. "They never know what's going on. It's amazing. Was your brother this dumb? I mean, not *dumb* dumb. I know he was smarter than you in middle school, but . . . wait, that came out wrong."

I put my hand on her knee. "Roshni," I said. "Stop and think, *then* talk." *Ooh, that felt good,* I thought.

She took a deep breath. "What I'm trying to say is, the boys have to get smarter, don't they?"

"Why?" I asked. "Why do they have to get smarter?"

"Well, like, look at Ryder. He learned how to talk to you. It only took him three years and a lockdown, but he finally got over his crush and—wait. I did not say that. I. Did. Not. Say. That."

"It's all right. I knew about that, and it's all over now."

"Okay. And then there's Christopher. He learned how to connect with people."

I glanced over at Christopher, who was sitting in the far back corner of the classroom, rolling balls of glue, and then forming them into little armies on top of the radiator.

"Well, sort of," she said. But honestly, it was true. I thought about how Christopher had defended me during and after the Lockdown Incident. He had learned. In a lot of ways, he might have turned himself into the bravest kid I knew.

"Plus, there's another thing. I know it's going to sound strange. In fact, I might be crazy. But I think the guys might not be, um . . ."

"What is it, Roshni?"

Her voice dropped to a whisper. "I think the guys might not be drawing as many of their ... uh ... *special pictures* all over everything."

I smiled. "You think *these guys* are growing out of *that?* No, Roshni, I'm pretty sure you're crazy."

25. Babes

Matthew's hands were clenched around the steering wheel as if he was trying to choke it to death, and his face was chalk white. He was muttering something under his breath, too quietly for me to hear the words. We were on our way to our first Dads' Dance rehearsal. I had thought I was going to be the nervous one, dancing with all the high school girls for the first time after being in the younger group all year, but Matthew was actually freaking out much more than I was.

"What are you saying, Matthew?" I asked.

He swallowed. It occurred to me that he might faint and swerve us off the road to our doom. *"Babes in leotards. Babes in leotards. Babes in leotards."*

"Oh, gross," I said.

"What? It's my chant of hope. I'm focusing on the positive."

"Oh, because dancing with me is so negative? Thanks."

"No, Claire. Like much of human existence, this isn't about you. The negative is that I don't know anything about dancing."

"So? You'll learn. You're always telling me how easy dancing is compared to your sports. Now's your chance to prove it. Besides, you're great at everything. Miss Nina will probably hire you by the end of the night. Then you can hang out with all the *babes in leotards* you want."

He didn't say anything more for a few minutes, until we were stopped in the parking lot of the dance school. Then he turned to me, and I saw his face was all scrunched up like it only gets when he is really, seriously nervous. I had seen the look the day he went to ask out his first girl, and the night before he took the SATs. "I'm serious. What if I *suck?*"

I suddenly understood how serious this really was for him, and how big a deal it was that he was doing it for me. The key to Matthew was that he always had to be in control. That was why he needed to be perfect at everything. I had heard my parents say that to each other a thousand times when they thought nobody could hear them. Now he had agreed to step into this completely different new situation where his baby sister knew more than he did.

I sighed. "Okay, listen. You aren't going to be good compared to the girls. But you're an amazing athlete. Of course you'll be better than a lot of the dads. Plus, everybody in the audience is really only looking at their own husband and daughter, or whatever, right?"

He nodded, slightly.

"Oh, and one other thing."

"What?"

"Babes. In leotards! Now come on."

. . . .

As soon as we stepped into the studio, Katherine and Alanna rushed over and kind of cocooned around me, which was really nice. The dads mingled with the other dads, the dancers stood around with each other, and Matthew stood there alone, looking like he wanted to die.

But then, suddenly, one of the older girls went over and put an arm around his shoulders. Another followed, and soon, my brother had a little harem of groupies. It was disgusting. I edged closer with Katherine and Alanna so I could hear what was going on.

A girl named Gabrielle said, "Matty, you have nothing to worry about! When they ask you to do a pirouette, you just have to go like this!" Then she stood on the tips of her toes and executed a flawless ballet turn.

Another, named Amber, said, "And if Miss Nina calls for a calypso, you just have to make sure you get a lot of hip rotation before you jump, like this!" Then she did a really good spinning jazz leap.

"Or," a third girl, named Elizabeth, chimed in, "you

might have to do some tap moves. Here's a shuffle ball change. Everybody?"

Suddenly, there were five girls tap-dancing all around my brother, all chanting, "Shuffle! Ball! Change!"

He still looked like he was going to die, but now I couldn't tell whether it was from fear or happiness. A moment later, when the girls all stopped dancing and started laughing, he said, "Wait. I'm not really going to have to do all this stuff, am I?"

And I realized: Even with the girls hanging all over him, he had still been mostly just worrying about messing up the dance.

"No," Elizabeth said. "My dad weighs two hundred and eighty pounds, and he's been doing this for the past three years. Do you think he'd keep coming back if he had to do leaps and big spin moves? Don't worry. All the dads have to do is, like, step and clap to the beat. You'll be fine. Unless you have one of the solos. Your sister didn't sign you up for a solo, did she?"

Matthew looked over at me. I just smiled.

. . . .

Of course Matthew didn't have a solo. His job was to stand on a fake surfboard and pretend he was trying not to fall off in the beginning when all the dads were onstage without the girls, to be my partner for a 1960s-type dance in the middle, and finally, to skip with me under a limbo bar at the end. By the end of the dress rehearsal, he was fine. Plus, the high school girls loved him. He was like their mascot.

On the way home that night, I thanked Matthew for being my partner.

"Hey," he said. "Babes in leotards." But I knew it was more than that.

. . . .

As soon as I got in the shower that night, I started crying. I didn't mean to. I hadn't felt it coming or anything. Just, all of a sudden, I was overwhelmed with sadness because Matthew and I were dancing together onstage, having fun, and my father's place had disappeared.

I mean, he was obviously still with us, at home, gaining muscle and strength. His reading was coming along, his mood swings were mostly gone, and his face wasn't even as droopy as it had been. He had even started sleeping in his own bedroom upstairs again. His recovery was better than we could have hoped for. But still, I was the one girl up there without her dad. It seemed wrong.

How was he going to feel, watching that from the audience?

Plus, there were so many stairs in the theater. And it was hard for him to walk sideways, so getting into his seat would be tough. AND I knew he hated speaking with people in public since the stroke, because he was embarrassed about his pauses and the words he couldn't remember.

It seemed almost mean of me to make him go.

When I was dry and dressed, I went into my parents' room. They were both there, sitting up in bed. "Dad," I said, "if you don't want to come to my recital, I would understand. I mean, I love you, and of course I want you there, but I know how hard stairs are for you, and..."

Then I burst out sobbing again, and put my head in my hands.

"Oh, Claire," he said, "Piggy." I looked through my fingers and saw that he was smiling. "I would...never...miss you dancing. If they have to wheel me in, I'll be there. You are my beautiful...uh, queen girl. Princess! I always want to see my princess up there in the lights. I love you."

My mom stood up, put her arms around me, and said, "Sweetheart, don't worry about anyone but yourself tomorrow. It's your big day. I'll get everyone where they need to be and they'll all do what they have to do. All you need to do is show up and dance. Okay? We've got this for you."

I nodded into her shoulder. Then I stood up straight, wiped my eyes, and sniffled.

"Tissue?" my dad asked, holding one out to me with an immensely pleased look on his face.

"What?" I asked.

"I've been trying to think of that word for weeks!" he replied. "Tissue! Tissue!"

I turned to go out and leave him with his victory, but then he asked me a question. "Hey, we're kind of dying . . . to know: Is your brother actually any good at dancing?"

"Sorry, Dad," I said. "Mom already bought the tickets. You'll just have to show up and see for yourselves."

June 15: Showtime

I'm waiting in the wings, watching all of the fathers dancing onstage. Well, all of the fathers except mine.

All of the other girls around me are whispering, pointing, giggling as their dads ham it up in the bright lights of the theater. There is booming surf music playing, and at the moment, half of the men are pretending to water-ski, while the rest are acting like lifeguards, throwing Frisbees around, hula-hooping, and even flying imaginary kites. It's incredibly dorky, but also incredibly sweet. My eyes burn, and I step back into the shadows a bit. I don't want anybody to see me tearing up, but it's hard to be inconspicuous as I dab at my face with the corner of my ridiculous tiki-girl skirt.

Alanna and Katherine notice, and drape their arms over my shoulders. This only makes the tears come faster. "I'm *fine*," I whisper, a bit more harshly than I mean to. They both pull away and give me that look—the sympathetic-but-doubtful one that everybody has been giving whenever I claim to be okay.

Alanna and Katherine let me go—or at least they do after I shrug their arms off my shoulders. And then

Matthew comes out onstage carrying a ridiculous ten-foot-long, red-sequined fake surfboard. He's decked out in loud orange surfer shorts with green palm trees all over them, plus a mismatched Hawaiian shirt, flip-flops, and huge black sunglasses.

When he drops the board down on the stage and starts gyrating his hips, all the high school girls in the wings start to whistle and cheer. Finally, for the first time all day, I smile. Logically, I know that the first half of the program is already over, so I must have already performed several of my dances, but everything before this moment has been a blur to me. All I have thought about until now—all I have thought about all year—is the Dads' Dance. Poor Dad. Poor Mom. Poor Matthew. Poor Me.

Well, at least Matthew—Matty—seems to be doing pretty well.

The music changes, and I realize that's my cue to run onstage and join my brother. "Nice moves," I whisper as he puts his arms around me.

"Did I do okay?" he asks.

"Didn't you hear the whistles?"

"I wasn't sure whether they were good whistles or bad whistles." He's actually looking sheepish about this. Well, at least my brother is humble while all the babes are cheering at him. I laugh.

Then we turn, and for a moment I am facing directly into the wings. With a shock, I realize my mother is standing there, just offstage. "Matthew, *Mom* is here."

"Duh."

"No, I mean she's in the wings. Right now. What if something happened to Dad? What if—"

"Shhh. I'm counting steps. You're going to mess me up. We're almost done anyway, right?"

We spin again.

"Besides," he says, "she's holding flowers. I'm sure it's fine."

"You're probably right," I say. But now my heart is pounding. I think through the rest of the number. There are something like seven dads with little solos, and then we're done and I can run off to see what's going on. That's only, like, fifty seconds? Forty?

But I can feel myself starting to panic. I am dancing on autopilot. This doesn't make any sense, but suddenly my only thought is, *Time is brain.*

And then it's the end of the dance. The last verse of the song leads into the final chorus. The solos are going on at the front of the stage, where I can't see them. Matthew and I are all the way in back. All the other girls are spinning around in their fathers' arms, getting ready for the big dip move that will be the climax of the number. There are only eight beats left.

Matthew spins me around so that I am facing away from him, and then gives me a gentle push in the small of my back. And—somehow—my father is there in front of me. The other girls and their dads must have known about this, because they have cleared a path between us. He steps toward me, slowly, with his cane in his strong left hand. Heel, toe, heel, toe. He's wearing tap shoes. This is the last solo!

I run to him with my arms outstretched. Just before I get there, my father drops his cane and holds out his hands. He clasps my right wrist with the good fingers of his left hand, and I reach down a bit to grab the still-weak fingers of his right. He smiles at me with his lopsided, oversize-kid grin.

This is what love is, I think. *Daddy was strong for me so that I could learn to be. Then I was strong for him until he could relearn his own strength. Now, here we are, strong together.*

As the final chord of the song vibrates through me, my father speaks. I can't hear his soft, breathy voice over the music and the swelling applause, but I can read his lips. He is saying this:

"Claire, I catching you."

Acknowledgments

When I sat down to do research for this book, I immediately realized I would need the services of a pretty broad panel of experts if I hoped to wrap my head around the tremendous complexities of stroke physiology and treatment, as well as the short- and long-term effects of strokes on patients and their families. I was incredibly lucky that the following individuals all gave unstintingly of their time and expertise, with great grace and aplomb.

Bil Rosen, BA, CEMSO, CTO, NRP, is a paramedic who literally wrote the manual on stroke response for emergency personnel. Lorettajo Kapinos, RN, BS, is an emergency-room nurse. Several parts of this novel, especially chapters five through eight, draw heavily on information that Bil and Lorettajo shared with me in interviews, and Bil also answered several follow-up questions via email months later.

My fellow children's author Lynn Plourde, who is a former speech-language therapist, raised several crucial questions about the time frame of stroke patients' language recovery. This led me to call my cousin, Joshua S. Brodkin, MD, DABR, who talked me through some of the technical aspects of whether my book's plot could work from a medical point of view. Every novelist should be sure to have an interventional radiologist in the family for just such an emergency.

Another author, my friend Ashley Hope Pérez, swooped in and saved me at the last minute by reading the manuscript and giving me feedback on various characters' development, as well as the overall flow of the plot. Ashley is a former public-school teacher, a top-notch young-adult novelist, and a university professor and researcher in the fields of world literature, Latin American literature, Latina/Latino literature, and narrative ethics. Being pals with an expert like her—who is willing to read and comment on a novel over the course of a single weekend—is a blessing.

Finally, my son's classmate Abigail Burnett, whose father, Ron, actually had a stroke when Abigail was in middle school, was kind enough to recount that experience to me in some detail, and while the type of stroke Ron had is medically quite different from the stroke portrayed in this book, hearing from a teen who had gone through an emotional event like the one I was describing was invaluable and affirming. Abigail is a treasure.

Any factual errors in this book made it into the manuscript despite the contributions of the above-named individuals, who went above and beyond to educate me.

On a different note, I have to give big props to my daughter's dance school, Art of Dance Studios in Bethlehem, Pennsylvania, both for everything she has learned there, and for actually having a Dads' Dance in the recital every year. After I finished writing *Falling Over Sideways*, I got my chance to be a Dancing Dad—and while I can't say my footwork was anything special, the experience was absolutely magical.

About the Author

Jordan Sonnenblick is the author of many acclaimed novels, including *Drums, Girls + Dangerous Pie*; *Notes from the Midnight Driver*; *Zen and the Art of Faking It*; *Curveball: The Year I Lost My Grip*; and *After Ever After*. He lives in Bethlehem, Pennsylvania, with his family and numerous musical instruments. You can find out a whole lot more about him at www.jordansonnenblick.com.

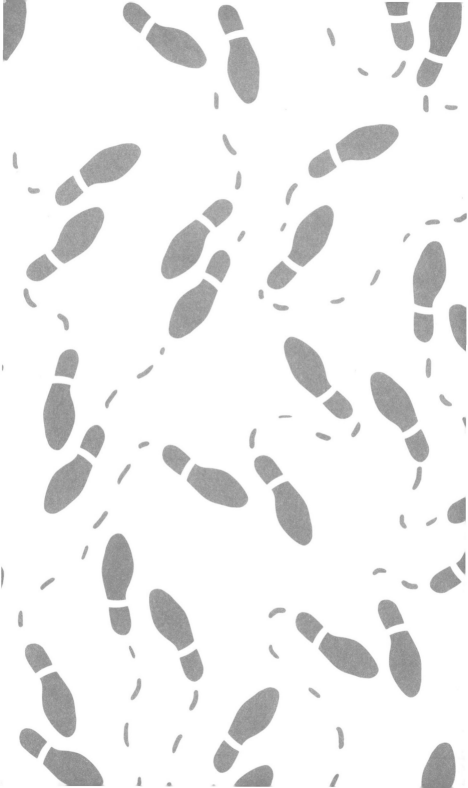

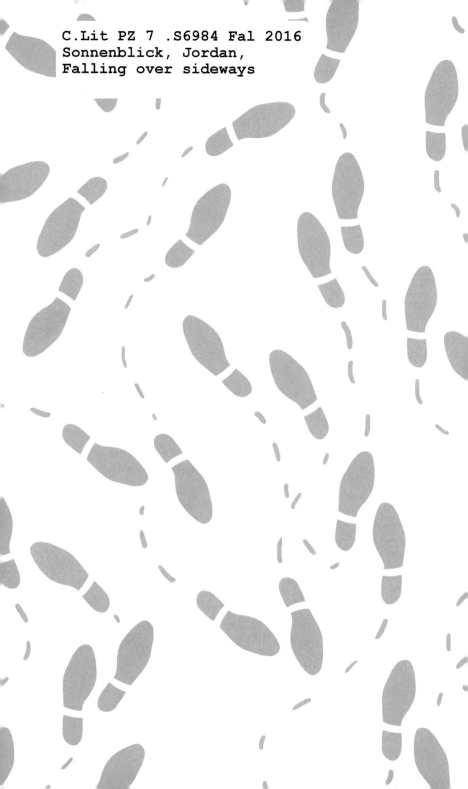